"Tyler, I'm Imagining You. You're Not Here, And I'm Not Seeing You!"

"I hope not," observed a third voice.

Amy whirled to find *Harry*. The expression in his eyes was bleak, resigned, and Amy knew he couldn't see Tyler.

"Do something!" Amy ordered Tyler frantically. "Show yourself, make a sound, tip over the table— *something!*"

"It's no use, Spud," Tyler said. "Nobody can see or hear me but you. To show myself to Harry would take so much energy that I'd probably short out or something."

Amy turned to Harry. "He's really here!" she cried. "Harry, I swear I'm not having delusions—Tyler is *right here!*"

Harry looked sad. "It's obvious that you're not ready for a new marriage, Amy." He collected his sweater. "I'll call you sometime."

"Now I know why they told me not to come back," Tyler muttered.

"Oh, shut up!" Amy yelled. She'd finally found new happiness, and it was walking out the door.

Books by Linda Lael Miller

Please address questions and book requests to:
Silhouette Reader Service
U.S.: 3010 Walden Ave., P.O. Box 1325, Buffalo, NY 14269
Canadian: P.O. Box 609, Fort Erie, Ont. L2A 5X3

LINDA LAEL MILLER

WILD ABOUT HARRY

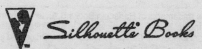

Published by Silhouette Books
America's Publisher of Contemporary Romance

For Jim Lang,
who married the girl with snowflakes in her hair,
thereby proving what a smart guy he really is.

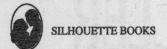

SILHOUETTE BOOKS

ISBN 0-373-48340-6

WILD ABOUT HARRY

One

Amy Ryan was safe in her bed, drifting in that place where slumber and wakefulness mesh into a tranquil twilight, when she distinctly felt someone grasp her big toe and wriggle it.

"Amy."

She groaned and pulled the covers up over her head. Two full years had passed since her handsome, healthy young husband, Tyler, had died on the operating table during a routine appendectomy. She *couldn't* be hearing his voice now.

"No," she murmured. "I refuse to have this dream again. I'm waking up right now!"

Amy's toe moved again, without orders from her brain. She swallowed, and her heart rate accelerated. Quickly, expecting to find eight-year-old Ashley's cat,

Rumpel, at the foot of the bed playing games, she reached out and snapped on the bedside lamp.

A scream rushed into her throat, coming from deep inside her, but she swallowed it. Even though Tyler was standing there, just on the other side of her blanket chest, Amy felt no fear.

She could never be afraid of Ty. No, what scared her was the explicit possibility that she was losing her mind at thirty-two years of age.

"This can't be happening," she whispered hoarsely, raising both hands to her face. From between her fingers, she could still see Tyler grinning that endearing grin of his. "I've been through counseling," she protested. "I've had grief therapy!"

Tyler chuckled and sat down on the end of the bed.

Amy actually felt the mattress move, so lifelike was this delusion.

"I'm quite real," Tyler said, having apparently read her mind. "At least, *real* is the closest concept you could be expected to understand."

"Oh, God," Amy muttered, reaching blindly for the telephone.

Tyler's grin widened. "This is a really lousy joke," he said, "but I can't resist. Who ya gonna call?"

Amy swallowed and hung up the receiver with an awkward motion of her hand. What *could* she say? Could she dial 911 and report that a ghost was haunting her bedroom?

If she did, the next stop would not be the *Twilight Zone,* it would be the mental ward at the nearest hospital.

Amy ran her tongue over dry lips, closed her eyes tightly, then opened them again, wide.

Tyler was still sitting there, his arms folded, charming smile in place. He had brown curly hair and mischievous brown eyes, and Amy had been in love with him since her freshman year at the University of Washington. She had borne him two children, eight-year-old Ashley and six-year-old Oliver, and the loss of her young husband had been the most devastating experience of Amy's life.

"What's happening to me?" Amy rasped, shoving a hand through her sleep-rumpled, shoulder-length brown hair.

Tyler scratched the back of his neck. He was wearing slacks and a blue cashmere cardigan over a tailored white shirt. "I look pretty solid, don't I?" He sounded proud, the way he used to when he'd won a particularly difficult case in court or beaten a colleague at racquet ball. "And let me tell you, being able to grab hold of your toe like that was no small feat, no pun intended."

Amy tossed back the covers, scrambled into the adjoining bathroom and frantically splashed cold water on her face. "It must have been the spicy cheese on the nachos," she told herself aloud, talking fast.

When she straightened and looked in the mirror, though, she saw Tyler's reflection. He was leaning against the doorjamb, his arms folded.

"Pull yourself together, Amy," he said good-naturedly. "It's taken me eighteen months to learn to do this, and I'm not real good at sustaining the energy yet. I could fade out at any time, and I have something important to say."

Amy turned and leaned back against the counter, her hands gripping the marble edge. She sank her teeth into her lower lip and wondered what Debbie would make of this when she told her about it. *If* she told her.

Your subconscious mind is trying to tell you something, her friend would say. Debbie was a counselor in a women's clinic, and she was working on her doctorate in psychology. *It's time to let go of Tyler and get on with your life.*

"Wh-what did you want to—to say?" Amy stammered. She was a little calmer now and figured this figment of her imagination might give her an important update on what was going on inside her head. There was absolutely no doubt, as far as she was concerned, that some of her gears were gummed up.

Tyler's gentle gaze swept her tousled hair, yellow cotton nightshirt and shapely legs with sad fondness.

"An old friend of mine is going to call you sometime in the next couple of days," he said after a long moment. "His name is Harry Griffith, and he runs a multinational investment company out of Australia. They're opening an office in Seattle, so Harry will be living here in the Puget Sound area part of the year. He'll get in touch to offer his condolences about me and pay off on a deal we made the last time we were together. You should get a pretty big check."

Amy certainly hadn't expected anything so specific. "Harry?" she squeaked. She vaguely remembered Tyler talking about him.

Tyler nodded. "We met when we were kids. We were both part of the exchange student program—he lived here for six months, and then I went down there and stayed with Harry and his mom for the same amount of time."

A lump had risen in Amy's throat, and she swallowed it. Yes, Harry Griffith. Tyler's mother, Louise, had spoken of him several times. "This is crazy," she said. "*I'm* crazy."

Her husband—or this mental *image* of her husband—smiled. "No, babe. You're a little frazzled, but you're quite sane."

"Oh, yeah?" Amy thrust herself away from the bathroom counter and passed Tyler in the doorway to stand next to the bed. "If I'm not one can short of a six-pack, how come I'm seeing somebody who's been dead for two years?"

Tyler winced. "Don't use that word," he said. "People don't really die, they just change."

Amy was feeling strangely calm and detached now, as though she were standing outside of herself. "I'll never eat nachos again," she said firmly.

Ty's gentle brown eyes twinkled with amusement. When he spoke, however, his expression was more serious. "You're doing very well, all things considered. You've taken good care of the kids and built a career for yourself, unconventional though it is. But there's one area where you're really blowing it, Spud."

Amy's eyes brimmed with tears. During the terrible days and even worse nights following Tyler's unexpected death, she'd yearned for just such an experience as this. She'd longed to see the man she'd loved so totally, to hear his voice. She'd even wanted to be called "Spud" again, although she'd hated the nickname while Tyler was alive.

She sniffled but said nothing, waiting for Tyler to go on.

He did. "There are women who can be totally fulfilled without a man in their lives. Give them a great job and a couple of kids and that's all they need. You aren't one of those women, Amy. You're not happy."

Amy shook her head, marveling. "Boy, when my subconscious mind comes up with a message, it's a doozy."

Tyler shrugged. "What can I say?" he asked reasonably. "Harry's the man for you."

"*You* were the man for me," Amy argued, and this time a tear escaped and slipped down her cheek.

He started toward her, as though he would take her into his arms, then, regretfully, he stopped. "That was then, Spud," he said, his voice gruff with emotion. "Harry's *now*. In fact, you're scheduled to remarry and have two more kids—a boy and a girl."

Amy's feeling of detachment was beginning to fade; she was trembling. This was all so crazy. "And this Harry guy is my one and only?" she asked with quiet derision. She was hurt because Tyler had started to touch her and then pulled back.

"Actually, there are several different men you could have fulfilled your destiny with. That architect you met three months ago, when you were putting together the deal for those condos on Lake Washington, for instance. Alex Singleton—the guy who replaced me in the firm, for another.'' He paused and shoved splayed fingers through his hair. "You're not cooperating, Spud.''

"Well, excuse me!'' Amy cried in a whispered yell, not wanting the children to wake and see her in the middle of a hallucination. "I *loved* you, Ty. You were everything to me. I'm not ready to care for anybody else!''

"Yes, you are,'' Tyler disagreed sadly. Quietly. "Get on with it, Amy. You're holding up the show.''

She closed her eyes for a moment, willing Tyler to disappear. When Amy looked again and found him gone, however, she felt all hollow and broken inside.

"Tyler?''

No answer.

Amy went slowly back to bed, switched out the light and lay down. "You're losing it, Ryan,'' she muttered to herself.

She tried to sleep, but images of Tyler kept invading her mind.

Amy recalled the first time they'd met, in the cafeteria at the University of Washington, when she'd been a lowly freshman and Tyler had been in his third year of law school. He'd smiled as he'd taken the chair across the table from Amy's, and she'd been so thoroughly, instantly besotted that she'd nearly fallen right into her lime Jell-O.

After that day, Amy and Tyler had been together every spare moment. Ty had taken her home to Mercer Island to meet his parents at Thanksgiving, and at Christmas he'd given her a three-carat diamond.

Amy had liked Tyler's parents immediately; they were so warm and friendly, and their gracious, expensive home practically vibrated with love and laughter. The contrast between the Ryans' family life and Amy's was total: Amy's father, one of the most famous heart surgeons in the country, was a distant, distracted sort of man, totally absorbed in his work. Although Amy knew her dad loved her, in his own workaholic way, he'd never been able to show it.

The free-flowing affection among the Ryans had quickly become vital to Amy, and she was still very close to them, even though Tyler had been gone for two years.

Alone in the bed where she and Tyler had once loved and slept and sometimes argued, Amy wept. "This isn't fair," she told the dark universe around her.

With the morning, however, came a sense of buoyant optimism. It seemed only natural to Amy that she'd had a vivid dream about Tyler; he was the father of her children and she'd loved him with her whole heart.

She was sticking frozen waffles in the toaster when Oliver and Ashley raced into the kitchen. During the school year she had trouble motivating them in the mornings, but now that summer had come, they were up and ready for day camp almost as soon as the morning paper hit the doorstep.

"Yo, Mom," Oliver said. He had a bandanna tied around his forehead and he was wearing shorts and a T-shirt with his favorite cartoon character on the front. "Kid power!" he whooped, thrusting a plastic sword into the air.

Ashley rolled her beautiful Tyler-brown eyes. "What a dope," she said. She was eight and had a lofty view of the world.

"Be careful, Oliver," Amy fretted good-naturedly. "You'll put out someone's eye with that thing." She put the waffles on plates and set them down on the table, then went to the refrigerator for the orange juice. "Look, you two, I might be home late tonight. If I can't get away, Aunt Charlotte will pick you up at camp."

Charlotte was Ty's sister and one of Amy's closest friends.

Ashley was watching Amy pensively as she poured herself a cup of coffee and joined the kids at the table.

"Were you talking to yourself last night, Mom?" the child asked in her usual straightforward way.

Amy was glad she was sitting down because her knees suddenly felt shaky. "I was probably just dreaming," she said, but the memory of Tyler standing there in their bedroom was suddenly vivid in her mind. He'd seemed so solid and so *real*.

Ashley's forehead crumpled in a frown, but she didn't pursue the subject any further.

Fortunately.

After Amy had rinsed the breakfast dishes, put them into the dishwasher and driven the kids to the park, where camp was held, she found herself watching for Tyler—waiting for him to come back.

When she'd showered and put on her best suit, a sleek creation of pale blue linen, along with a matching patterned blouse, she sat on the edge of her bed and stared at the telephone for what must have been a full five minutes. Then she dialed her best friend's number.

"Debbie?"

"Hi, Amy," Debbie answered, sounding a little rushed. "If this is about lunch, I'm open. Twelve o'clock at Ivar's?"

Amy bit her lower lip for a moment. "I can't, not today...I have appointments all morning. Deb—"

Debbie's voice was instantly tranquil, all sense and sound of hurry gone. "Hey, you sound kind of funny. Is something wrong?"

"It might be," Amy confessed.

"Go on."

"I dreamed about Tyler last night, and it was ultra-real, Debbie. I wasn't lying in bed with my eyes closed—I was standing up, walking around—we had an in-depth conversation!"

Debbie's voice was calm, but then, she was a professional in the mental health field. It would take more than Amy's imaginary encounter with her dead husband to shock this woman. "Okay. What about?"

Amy was feeling sillier by the moment. "It's so dumb."

"Right. So tell me anyway."

"He said I was going to meet—this friend of his—Harry somebody. Who names people Harry in this day and age? I'm supposed to fall in love with this guy, marry him and have two kids."

"Before nightfall?" Debbie retorted, without missing a beat.

"Practically. Ty implied that I've been holding up some celestial plan by keeping to myself so much!"

Debbie sighed. "This is one that could be worked out in a fifteen-minute segment of the *Donahue* show, Ryan. You're a healthy young woman, and you haven't been with a man since Ty, and you're lonely, physically and emotionally. If you want to talk this out with somebody, I could give you a name—"

Amy was already shaking her head. "No," she interrupted, "that's all right. I feel foolish enough discussing this with my dearest friend. I don't think I'm up to stretching out on a couch and telling all to some strange doctor."

"Still—"

"I'll be all right, Deb," Amy broke in again, this time a little impatiently. She didn't know what she'd wanted her friend to say when she told her about Tyler's "visit," but she felt let down. She hung up quickly and then dashed off to her first meeting of the day.

Amy often marveled that she'd made such a success of her business, especially since she'd dropped out of school when Tyler passed the bar exam and devoted herself entirely to being a wife and mother.

She'd been totally happy doing those things and hadn't even blushed to admit to having no desire to work outside the home.

After Tyler's death, however, the pain and rage had made her so restless that staying home was impossible. She'd alternated between fits of sobbing and periods of wooden silence, and after a few weeks she'd gone numb inside.

One night, very late, she'd seen a good-looking, fast-talking man on television, swearing by all that was holy that she, too, could build a career in real estate trading and make a fortune.

Amy had enough money to last a lifetime, between Tyler's life insurance and savings and her maternal grandmother's trust fund, but the idea of a challenge, of building something, appealed to her. In fact, on some level it resurrected her. Here was something to *do*, something to keep her from smothering Ashley and Oliver with motherly affection.

She'd called a toll-free number and ordered a set of tapes and signed up for a seminar, as well.

The tapes arrived and Amy absorbed them. The voice was pleasant and the topic complicated enough that she had to concentrate, which meant she had brief respites from thinking about Tyler. Under any other circumstances, Amy would not have had the brass to actually do the things suggested by the tapes and seminar, but all her normal inhibitions had been frozen inside her, like small animals trapped in a sudden Ice Age.

She'd started buying and selling and wheeling and dealing, and she'd been successful at it.

Still, she thought miserably as she drove toward her meeting, Tyler had been right, she wasn't happy. Now that the numbness had worn off, all those old needs and hurts were back in full force and being a real estate magnate wasn't fulfilling them.

Harry Griffith smiled grimly to himself as he took off his headphones and handed them to his copilot, Mark Ellis. "Here you are, mate," he said. "Bring her in for me, will you?"

Mark nodded as he eagerly took over the controls, and Harry left the cockpit and proceeded into the main section of the private jet. Often it was filled with business people, hangers-on and assorted bimbos, but that day Harry and Mark were cutting through the sky alone.

He went on to the sumptuous bedroom, unknotting his silk tie with one hand as he closed the door with the other. He'd had a meeting in San Francisco, but now he could change into more casual clothes.

With a sigh Harry pulled open a few drawers and took out a lightweight cable-knit sweater and jeans, still thinking of his friend. He hadn't been present for Ty's services two years before. He'd been in the outback, at one of the mines, and by the time he'd returned to Sydney and learned about Tyler's death, it was three weeks after the fact.

He'd sent flowers to Tyler's parents, who'd been like a second mother and father to him ever since his first visit to the states, and to the pretty widow. Harry had never seen Amy Ryan or her children, except on the front of the Christmas cards he always received from them, and he hadn't known what to say to her.

It had been a damn shame, a man like Tyler dying in his prime like that, and Harry could find no words of comfort inside himself.

Now, however, he had business with Tyler's lovely lady, and he would have to open this last door that protected his own grief and endure whatever emotions might be set free in the process.

Harry tossed aside his tie and began unfastening his cuff links. Maybe he'd even go and stand by Tyler's grave for a while, tell his friend he was a cheeky lot for bailing out so early in the game that way.

He pulled the sweater on over his head, replaced his slacks with jeans, then stood staring at himself in the mirror. Like the bed, chairs and bureau, it was bolted down.

Where Tyler had been handsome in an altar-boy sort of way, Harry was classically so, with dark hair, indigo-blue eyes and an elegant manner. He regarded his exceptional looks as tools, and he'd used them without compunction, every day of his life, to get what he wanted.

Or most of what he wanted, that is. He'd never had a real family of his own, the way Tyler had. God knew, Madeline hadn't even tried to disguise herself as a wife, and she'd sent the child she'd borne her first husband to boarding school in Switzerland. Madeline hadn't wanted to trouble herself with a twelve-year-old daughter, and Eireen's letters and phone calls had been ignored more than answered.

Harry felt sick, remembering. He'd tried to establish a bond with the child on her rare holidays in Australia, but while Madeline hadn't wanted to be bothered with the little girl, she hadn't relished the idea of sharing her, either.

Then, after another stilted Christmas, Madeline had decided she needed a little time on the "the continent," and would therefore see Eireen as far as Zurich. Their plane had gone down midway between New Zealand and the Fiji Islands, and there had been no survivors.

Harry had not wept for his wife—the emotion he'd once mistaken for love had died long before she did—but he'd cried for that bewildered child who'd never been permitted to love or be loved.

Later, when Tyler had died, Harry had gotten drunk—something he had never done before or since—and stayed that way for three nightmarish days. It had been an injustice of cosmic proportions that a man like Tyler Ryan, who had had everything a man could dream of, should be sent spinning off the world that way, like a child from a carnival ride that turned too fast.

"Mr. Griffith?"

Mark's voice, coming over the intercom system, startled Harry. "Yes?" he snapped, pressing a button on the instrument affixed to the wall above his bed, a little testy at the prospect of landing in Seattle.

"We're starting our descent, sir. Would you like to come back and take the controls?"

"You can handle it," Harry answered, removing his finger from the button. He thought of Tyler's parents and the big house on Mercer Island where he'd spent some of the happiest times of his life. "You can handle it," he repeated gravely, even though Mark couldn't hear him now. "The question is, can I?"

Amy had had a busy day, but she'd managed to finish work on time to pick up Oliver and Ashley at day camp, and she was turning hot dogs on the grill in her stove when the telephone rang.

Oliver answered with his customary "Yo!" He listened to the caller with ever-widening eyes and then thrust the receiver in Amy's direction. "I think it's that guy from the movies!" he shouted.

Amy frowned, crossed the room and took the call. "Hello?"

"Mrs. Ryan?" The voice was low, melodic and distinctly Australian. "My name is Harry Griffith, and I was a friend of your husband's—"

The receiver slipped from Amy's hand and clattered against the wall. Harry Griffith? *Harry Griffith!* The man Tyler had mentioned in her dream the night before.

"Mom!" Ashley cried, alarmed. She'd learned, at entirely too young an age, that tragedy almost always took a person by surprise.

"It's okay, sweetheart," Amy said hastily, snatching up the telephone with one hand and pulling her daughter close with the other. "Hello? Mr. Griffith?"

"Are you all right?" he asked in that marvelous accent.

Amy leaned against the counter, not entirely trusting her knees to support her, and drew in a deep breath. "I'm fine," she lied.

"I don't suppose you remember me..."

Amy didn't remember Harry Griffith, except from old photographs and things Tyler had said, and she couldn't recall seeing him at the funeral. "You knew Tyler," she said, closing her eyes against a wave of dizziness.

"Yes," he answered. His voice was gentle and somehow encouraging, like a touch. "I'd like to take you out for dinner tomorrow night, if you'll permit."

If you'll permit. The guy talked like Cary Grant in one of those lovely old black-and-white movies on the Nostalgia Channel. "Ah—well—maybe you should just come here. Say seven o'clock?"

"Seven o'clock," he confirmed. There was brief pause, then, "Mrs. Ryan? I'm very sorry—about Tyler, I mean. He was one of the best friends I ever had."

Amy's eyes stung, and her throat felt thick. "Yes," she agreed. "I felt pretty much the same way about him. I—I'll see you at seven tomorrow night. Do you have the address?"

"Yes," he answered, and then the call was over.

It took Amy so long to hang up the receiver that Oliver finally pulled it from her hand and replaced it on the hook.

"Who was that?" Ashley asked. "Is something wrong with Grampa or Gramma?"

"No, sweetheart," Amy said gently, bending to kiss the top of Ashley's head, where her rich brown hair was parted. "It was only a friend of your daddy's. He's coming by for dinner tomorrow night."

"Okay," Ashley replied, going back to the table.

Amy took the hot dogs from the grill and served them, but she couldn't eat because her stomach was jumping back and forth between its normal place and her windpipe. She went outside and sat at the picnic table in her expensive suit, watching as the sprinkler turned rhythmically, making its *chicka-chicka* sound.

She tried to assemble all the facts in her mind, but they weren't going together very well.

Last night she'd dreamed—only *dreamed*—that Tyler had appeared in their bedroom. Amy could ascribe that to the spicy Mexican food she'd eaten for dinner the previous night, but what about the fact that he'd told her his friend Harry Griffith would call and ask to see her? Could it possibly be a wild coincidence and nothing more?

She pressed her fingers to her temples. The odds against such a thing had to be astronomical, but the only other explanation was that she was psychic or something. And Amy knew that wasn't true.

If she'd had any sort of powers, she would have foreseen Tyler's death. She would have *done* something about it, warned the doctors, anything.

Presently, Amy pulled herself together enough to go back inside the house. She ate one hot dog, for the sake of appearances, then went to her bathroom to shower and put on shorts and a tank top.

Oliver and Ashley were in the family room, arguing over which program to watch on TV, when Amy joined them. Unless the exchanges threatened to turn violent, she never interfered, believing that children needed to learn to work out their differences without a parent jumping in to referee.

The built-in mahogany shelves next to the fireplace were lined with photo albums, and Amy took one of the early volumes down and carried it to the couch.

There she kicked off her shoes and sat cross-legged on the cushion, opening the album slowly, trying to prepare herself for the inevitable jolt of seeing Tyler smiling back at her from some snapshot.

After flipping the pages for a while, acclimating herself for the millionth time to a world that no longer contained Tyler Ryan, she began to look closely at the pictures.

Two

The next day, on the terrace of a busy waterfront restaurant, Amy tossed a piece of sourdough bread to one of the foraging sea gulls and sighed. "For all I know," she confided to her best friend, "Harry Griffith is an ax murderer. And I've invited him to dinner."

Debbie's eyes sparkled with amusement. "How bad can he be?" she asked reasonably. "Tyler liked him a lot, didn't he? And your husband had pretty good judgment when it came to human nature."

Amy nodded, pushing away what remained of her spinach and almond salad. "Yes," she admitted grudgingly.

A waitress came and refilled their glasses of iced tea, and Debbie added half a packet of sweetener to hers, stirring vigorously. "So what's really bugging you?

That you saw Tyler in a dream and he said a guy named Harry Griffith would come into your life, and now that's about to come true?"

"Wouldn't that bother you?" Amy countered, exasperated. "Don't look now, Deb, but things like this don't happen every day!"

Debbie looked thoughtful. "The subconscious mind is a fantastic thing," she mused. "'We don't even begin to comprehend what it can do."

Amy took a sip of her tea. "You think I *projected* Tyler from some shadowy part of my brain, don't you?"

"Yes," Debbie answered matter-of-factly.

"Okay, fine. I can accept that theory. But how do you account for the fact that Tyler mentioned Harry Griffith, specifically and by name? How could that have come from my subconscious mind, when I never actually knew the man?"

Debbie shrugged. "There were pictures in the albums, and I'm sure Tyler probably talked about him often. I suppose his parents must have talked about the guy sometimes, too. We pick up subliminal information from the people around us all the time."

Her friend's theory made sense, but Amy was still unconvinced. If she'd only conjured an image of Tyler for her own purposes, she would have had him hold her, kiss her, tell her the answers to cosmic mysteries. She would never have spent those few precious moments together talking about some stranger from Australia.

Amy shook her head and said nothing.

Debbie reached out to take her hand. "Listen, Amy, what you need is a vacation. You're under a lot of stress and you haven't resolved your conflicts over Tyler's death. Park the kids with Tyler's parents and go somewhere where the sun's shining. Sunbathe, spend money with reckless abandon, *live* a little."

Amy recalled briefly that she'd always wanted to visit Australia, then pushed the thought from her mind. A trip like that wouldn't be much fun all by herself. "I have work to do," she hedged.

"Right," Debbie answered. "You really need the money, don't you? Tyler had a whopping insurance policy, and then there was the trust fund from your grandmother. Add to that the pile you've made on your own with this real estate thing—"

"All right," Amy interrupted. "You're right. I'm lucky, I have plenty of money. But work fills more than just financial needs, you know."

Debbie's look was wryly indulgent, and she didn't speak at all. She just tapped the be-ringed fingers of her right hand against the upper part of her left arm, waiting for Amy to dig herself in deeper.

"Listen," Amy whispered hoarsely, not wanting diners at the neighboring tables to overhear, "I know what you're really saying, okay? I'm young. I'm healthy. I should be...*having sex* with some guy. Well, in case you haven't noticed, the smart money is on celibacy these days!"

"I'm not telling you to go out and seduce the first man you meet, Amy," Debbie said frankly, making no apparent effort to moderate her tone. "What I'm really saying is that you need to stop mourning Tyler and *get on with your life.*"

Amy snatched up her check, reached for her purse and pushed back her chair. "Thanks," she snapped, hot color pooling in her cheeks. "You've been a real help!"

"Amy..."

"I have a meeting," Amy broke in. And then she walked away from the table without even looking back.

Debbie caught up to her at the cash register. "My brother has a condo at Lake Tahoe," she persisted gently. "You could go there for a few days and just walk along the shore and look at the trees and stuff. You could visit the house they used in *Bonanza.*"

Despite her nervous and irritable mood, Amy had to smile. "You make it sound like a pilgrimage," she replied, picking up her credit card receipt and placing it neatly in a pocket of her brown leather purse. "Shall I burn candles and say, 'Spirits of Hoss, Adam and Little Joe, show me the way'?"

Now it was Debbie who laughed. "Your original hypothesis was correct, Ryan. You are indeed crazy."

It was an uncommonly sunny day, even for late June, and the sidewalks were crowded with tourists. Amy spoke softly, "I'm sorry, Deb. I was really a witch in there."

Debbie grinned. "True, but being a friend means knowing somebody's faults and liking them anyway. And to show you I do have some confidence in your reasoning processes, expect my cousin Max over tonight." She paused to think a moment, then her pretty face was bright with inspiration. "Max will wear coveralls and pretend to be fixing the dishwasher or something. That way, there'll be a man in the house, in case this Griffith guy really is an ax murderer, but Mr. Australia will never guess you were nervous about having him over."

Amy wasn't crazy about the idea, but she had neither the time nor the energy to try to talk Debbie out of it. She had an important meeting scheduled and, after that, some shopping to do at the Pike Place Market.

"I'll call you tomorrow," Amy promised, as the two women went in their separate directions.

Because she didn't know whether to go with elegant or simple and typically American, Amy settled on a combination of the two and bought fresh salmon steaks to be seasoned, wrapped in foil and cooked on the backyard barbecue. She made a potato salad as well, and set out chocolate éclairs from an upscale bakery for dessert.

She was setting the picnic table with good silver when a jolting sensation in the pit of her stomach alerted her to the fact that she wasn't alone.

Amy looked up, expecting to see Debbie's cousin Max or perhaps even Tyler. Instead, she found herself tumbling end over end into the bluest pair of eyes she'd ever seen.

"Hello," the visitor said.

Oliver, who had apparently escorted their guest from the front door, was clearly excited. "He sounds just like Crocodile Dundee when he talks, doesn't he, Mom?" he crowed.

The dark-haired man was incredibly handsome—Amy recalled seeing his picture once or twice—and he smiled down at Oliver with quiet warmth. "We're mates, me and Mick Dundee," he said in a very thick and rhythmic down-under accent.

"Wow!" Oliver shouted.

The visitor chuckled and ruffled the boy's hair. Then he noticed Ashley, who was standing shyly nearby, holding her beloved cat and looking up at the company with wide eyes.

"My name is Ashley Ryan," she said solemnly. "And this is my cat, Rumpel. That's short for Rumpelteazer."

Amy was about to intercede—after all, this man hadn't even had a chance to introduce himself yet—but before she could, he reached out and patted Rumpel's soft, striped head.

"Ah," he said wisely. "This must be a Jellicle cat, then."

Ashley's answering smile was sudden and so bright as to be blinding. She'd named Rumpel for one of the characters in the musical *Cats:* Tyler had taken her to see the show at Seattle's Paramount Theater several months before his death. Ever since, the play had served as a sort of connection between Ashley and the father she had loved so much.

"Harry Griffith," the man said, solemnly offering his hand to Ashley in greeting. He even bowed, ever so slightly, and his mouth quirked at one corner as he gave Amy a quick, conspiratorial glance. "I'm very glad to meet you, Ashley Ryan."

Amy felt herself spinning inwardly, off balance, like a washing machine with all the laundry wadded up on one side of the tub. She reached out, resting one hand against the edge of the picnic table.

Harry's indigo eyes came back to her face, and she thought she saw tender amusement in their depths. He wore his expensive clothes with an air only a rich and accomplished man could have managed, and Amy concluded that he was used to getting reactions from the woman he encountered.

It annoyed her, and her voice was a little brisk when she said, "Hello, Mr. Griffith."

His elegant mouth curved slightly, and the ink-blue eyes danced. "I'm very glad to make your acquaintance, Mrs. Ryan. But since Tyler was one of my best friends, I'd be more comfortable having you call me Harry."

"Harry." The name came out of Amy's mouth sounding like primitive woman's first attempt at speech. "My name is Amy."

"I know," Harry answered, and, oddly, his voice affected Amy like a double dose of hot-buttered rum, finding its way into her veins and coursing through her system. Leaving her dizzy.

"S-sit down," Amy said, gesturing toward the picnic table.

"I'd like that," Harry replied. "But first I'd better tell you that there's a man in coveralls out front, ringing your doorbell."

Debbie's cousin Max, no doubt. Although she knew intuitively that she wouldn't need protection from a make-believe dishwasher repairman, Amy was relieved to have something to do besides standing there feeling as if she were about to topple over the edge of a precipice.

"Please," Amy said. "Make yourself at home. I'll be right back." As she hurried into the house, she couldn't help remembering what Tyler had said, that she was meant to marry Harry Griffith and have two children by him. She was glad no one else could possibly know about the quicksilver, heated fantasies *that* idea had produced.

Sure enough, she found Debbie's cousin peering through the glass in the front door.

She opened it. "Max? Listen, you really don't need—"

"Can't be too careful," the balding middle-aged man said, easing past Amy with his toolbox in hand. Then, in a much louder voice, he added, "Just show me to your dishwasher, and I'll make short order of that leak."

"You do understand that the dishwasher isn't broken?" Amy inquired in a whisper as she led the way to the kitchen.

He replied with a wink, set his toolbox in the center of the table, took out a screwdriver and went right to work.

Amy drew three or four deep breaths and let them out slowly before pushing open the screen door and facing Harry Griffith again.

He had already won over both the kids; Ashley was beaming with delight as he pushed her higher and higher in the tire swing Tyler had hung from a branch of the big maple tree a few years before. Oliver was waiting his turn with uncharacteristic patience.

Amy had a catch in her throat as she watched the three of them together. Until that moment, she'd managed to kid herself that she could be both mother and father to her children, but they were blossoming under Harry's attention like flowers long-starved for water and sunlight.

She watched them for a few bittersweet moments, then went to the grill to check the salmon. The sound of her children's laughter lifted her heart and, at the same time, filled her eyes with tears.

Amy was drying her cheek with the back of one hand when both Oliver and Ashley raced past, arguing in high-pitched voices.

"I'll do it!" Oliver cried.

"No, *I* want to!" Ashley replied.

Rumpel wisely took refuge under the rhododendron beside the patio.

"What...?" Amy turned to see Harry Griffith standing directly behind her.

He shrugged and grinned in a way that tugged at her heart. "I didn't mean to cause a disruption," he said. "I guess I should have gone back to the car for the cake myself, instead of sending the kids for it."

Amy sniffled. "Did you know Tyler very well?" she asked.

Harry was standing so close that she could smell his after-shave and the fabric softener in his sweater, and together, those two innocent scents caused a virtual riot in her senses. "We spent the better part of a year together," he answered. "And we kept in touch, as much as possible, after high school and college." He paused, taking an apparent interest in the fragrant white lilacs clambering over the white wooden arbor a few yards away. "I probably knew Ty better than most people—" Harry's gaze returned to her, and her heart welcomed it "—and not as well as you did."

Smoothly, one hand in the pocket of his tailored gray slacks, Harry reached out and, with the pad of his thumb, wiped a stray tear from just beneath Amy's jawline. Before she could think of anything to say, the kids returned, each carrying one end of a white bakery box.

Harry thanked them both in turn, making it sound as though they'd smuggled an important new vaccine across enemy lines.

"I guess we'd better eat," Amy said brightly. "It's getting late."

Oliver and Ashley squeezed in on either side of Harry, leaving Amy alone on the opposite bench of the picnic table. She felt unaccountably jealous of their attention, suddenly wanting it all for herself.

"Mom says you and Dad were buddies," Oliver announced, once the salmon and potato salad and

steamed asparagus had been dealt with. He was looking expectantly at their guest.

Harry put his hand on Oliver's wiry little shoulder.
"The very best of buddies," he confirmed. "Tyler was
one of the finest men I've ever known."

Oliver's freckled face fairly glowed with pride and
pleasure, but in the next instant he looked solemn
again. "Sometimes," he confessed, with a slight trace
of the lisp Amy had thought he'd mastered, "I can't
remember him too well. I was only four when
he...when he died."

"Maybe I can help you recall," Harry said gently,
taking a wallet from the hip pocket of his slacks and
carefully removing an old, often-handled snapshot.
"This was taken over at Lake Chelan, right here in
Washington State."

Ashley and Oliver nearly bumped heads in their eagerness to look at the picture of two handsome young
men grinning as they held up a pair of giant rainbow
trout for the camera.

"Your dad and I were seventeen then." Harry
frowned thoughtfully. "We were out in the rowboat
that day, as I recall. Your Aunt Charlotte was annoyed with us and she swam ashore, taking the oars
with her. It was humiliating, actually. An old lady in
a paddleboat had to come out and tow us back to the
dock."

Amy chuckled, feeling a sweet warmth flood her
spirit as she remembered Ty telling that same story.

After they'd had some of Harry's cake—they completely scorned the éclairs—Amy sent both her pro-

testing children into the house to get ready for bed. She and Harry remained outside at the picnic table, even after the sun went down and the mosquitoes came and the breeze turned chilly.

"I'm sorry I didn't make it to Ty's funeral," he said, after one long and oddly comfortable silence. "I was in the outback, and didn't find out until some three weeks after he'd passed on."

"I wouldn't have known whether you were there or not. I was in pretty much of a muddle." Amy's voice went a little hoarse as the emotional backwash of that awful day flooded over her.

Harry ran his fingers through his hair, the first sign of agitation Amy had seen him reveal. "*I* knew the difference," he said. "I needed to say goodbye to Tyler. Matter of fact, I needed to bellow at him that he had a hell of a nerve going and dying that way when he was barely thirty-five."

"I was angry with him, too," Amy said softly. "One day he was fine, the next he was in the hospital. The doctor said it would be a routine operation, nothing to worry about, and when I saw Ty before surgery, he was making jokes about keeping his appendix in a jar." She paused, and a smile faltered on her mouth, then fell away. She went on to describe what happened next, even though she was sure Harry already knew the tragic details, because for some reason she needed to say it all.

"Tyler had some kind of reaction to the anesthetic and went into cardiac arrest. The surgical team tried everything to save him, of course, but they couldn't get his heart beating again. He was just...gone."

Harry closed warm, strong fingers around Amy's hand. "I'm sorry," he said.

One of the patio doors slid open, and Amy looked up, expecting to see Ashley or Oliver standing there, making a case for staying up another hour. Instead, she was jolted to find cousin Max, complete with coveralls and toolbox.

Amy was horrified that she'd left the man kneeling on the kitchen floor throughout the evening, half his body swallowed up by an appliance that didn't even need repairing. "Oh, Max...I'm sorry, I—"

Max waggled a sturdy finger at her. "Everything's fine now, Mrs. Ryan." He looked at Harry and wriggled his eyebrows, clearly stating, without another word, that he had sized up the dinner guest and decided he was harmless.

In Amy's opinion, Max couldn't have been more wrong. Harry Griffith was capable of making her feel things, remember things, want things. And that made him damn dangerous.

"Mr. Griffith was just leaving," she said suddenly. "Maybe you could walk him to his car."

Harry tossed her a curious smile, gave his head one almost imperceptible shake and stood. "I've some business to settle with you," he said to Amy, "but I guess it will keep until morning."

Amy closed her eyes for a moment, shaken again. She knew what that business was without asking, because Tyler had told her. This was all getting too spooky.

Harry was already standing, so Amy stood, too.

"It's been a delightful evening," he said. "Thank you for everything."

His words echoed in Amy's mind as he walked away to join Max. *It's been a delightful evening.* She wasn't used to Harry's elegant, formal way of speaking: Tyler would have swatted her lightly on the bottom and said, *Great potato salad, babe. How about rubbing my back?*

"You're making me sound like a redneck," a familiar voice observed, and Amy whirled to see Tyler sitting in the tire swing, grinning at her in the light of the rising moon.

She raised one hand, as if to summon Harry or Max back, so that someone else could confirm the vision, then let it fall back to her side. "It's true," she said, stepping closer to the swing and keeping her voice down, so the kids wouldn't think she was talking to herself again. "Don't deny it, Ty. You enjoyed playing king of the castle. In fact, sometimes you did everything but swing from vines and yodel while beating on your chest with both fists."

Tyler, or his reflection, raised one eyebrow. "Okay, so I was a little macho sometimes. But I loved you, Spud. I was a good provider and a faithful husband."

Instinct, not just wishful thinking, told Amy that Ty's claim was true. He'd been the ideal life partner, except that he'd thrown the game before they'd even reached halftime.

"Go ahead, gloat," Amy said, folding her arms. "You told me Harry Griffith would turn up, and he did. And he said something about discussing business with me tomorrow, so you're batting a thousand."

Tyler grinned again, looking cocky. "You thought you were dreaming, didn't you?"

"Actually, no," Amy said. "It's more likely that you're some sort of projection of my subconscious mind."

"Oh, yeah?" Tyler made the swing spin a couple of times, the way he'd done on so many other summer nights, before he'd single-handedly brought the world to an end by dying. Somewhere in that library of albums inside the house, Amy had a picture of him holding an infant Ashley on his lap while they both turned in a laughing blur. "How could your subconscious mind have known Harry was about to show up?"

Amy shrugged. "There are a lot of things going on in this world that we don't fully understand."

"You can say that again," Tyler said, a little smugly.

He still couldn't resist an opportunity to be one up on the opposition in any argument, Amy reflected, with affection and acceptance. It was the lawyer in him. "Debbie's theory is that you represent some unspoken wish for love and romance."

Tyler laughed. "Unspoken, hell. I'm telling you straight out, Spud. You're not going to find a better guy than Harry, so you'd better grab him while you've got the chance."

Only then did Amy realize she hadn't felt an urge to fling herself at Tyler, the way she had before. The revelation made her feel sad. "Doesn't it make you even slightly jealous to think of me married to someone else?"

Amy regretted the words the instant she'd spoken them, because a bereft expression shadowed Tyler's handsome features for several moments.

"Yes," he admitted gruffly, "but this is about letting go and moving on. Think of me as a ghost, or a figment of your imagination, whatever works for you. As long as you get the message and stop marking time, it doesn't matter."

"*Are* you a ghost?"

Tyler sighed. "Yes and no."

"Spoken like a true lawyer."

He reached out one hand for her, as he would have done before, but once again he pulled back. He didn't smile at Amy's comment, either. "I'm not a specter, forced to wander the earth and rattle chains like in the stories they used to tell at summer camp," he told her. "But I'm not an image being beamed out of your deeper mind, either. I'm just as real as you are."

Amy swallowed hard. "I don't understand!" she wailed in a low voice, frustrated.

"You're not supposed to," Tyler assured her gently. "There's no need for you to understand."

Amy stepped closer, needing to touch Tyler, but between one instant and the next he was gone. No fade-out, no flash, nothing. He was there and then he wasn't.

"Tyler?" Amy whispered brokenly.

"Mom?" Ashley's voice made Amy start, and she turned to see her daughter standing only a few feet behind her, wearing cotton pajamas and carrying her favorite doll. "Did Mr. Harry go home?"

Apparently Ashley hadn't heard her mother talking to thin air, and Amy was relieved. She reached out to stop the tire swing, which was still swaying back and forth in the night air.

"Yes, sweetheart," she said. "He's really a nice man, isn't he?"

Ashley nodded gravely. "I like to listen to him talk. I wish *he* was still here, so he could tell us a kangaroo story."

"Maybe he doesn't know any," she suggested, distracted. If Tyler had known what she was thinking earlier, had he also discerned that his widow felt a powerful attraction to one of his best friends?

"Sure, he does," Ashley said confidently as they stepped into the kitchen together. Amy closed and locked the sliding door. "Did you know they have yellow signs in Australia, with the silhouette of a kangaroo on them—like the Deer Crossing signs here?"

Amy turned off the outside lights and checked to make sure all the leftovers had been put away. The dishwasher showed no signs of Max's exploratory surgery. "No, sweetheart," she said, standing at the sink now and staring out the window at the tire swing. It was barely visible in the deepening darkness. "I didn't know that. I guess it makes sense, though. Off to bed now."

"What about the story?"

Amy felt tears sting her eyes as she stared out at the place where Tyler had been. That was what her life was these days, it seemed, just a place where Tyler had been.

Harry sat on the stone bench beside Tyler's fancy marble headstone, his chin propped in one palm. "Damn it, man," he complained, "you didn't tell me she was beautiful. You didn't say anything about the warm way she laughs, or those golden highlights in her hair." He sighed heavily. "All right," he conceded. "I guess you did say she was a natural wonder, but I thought you were just talking. Even the Christmas cards didn't prepare me..."

He stood, tired of sitting, and paced back and forth at the foot of Tyler's grave. It didn't bother him, being in a cemetery at night. He wasn't superstitious and, besides, he'd been needing this confrontation with Tyler for a good long time.

"You might have stuck around a few more years, you know!" he muttered, shoving one hand through his usually perfect hair. "There you were with that sweet wife, those splendid children, a great career. And what did you do? In the name of God, Tyler, why didn't you *fight?*"

The only answer, of course, was a warm night wind and the constant chirping of crickets.

Harry stopped his pacing and stood with one foot braced against the edge of the bench, staring down at the headstone with eyes that burned a little. "All right, mate," he said softly, hoarsely. "I know you probably had your reasons for not holding on longer—and that's not to say I won't be wanting an accounting when I catch up with you. In the meantime, what's really got under my skin is, well, it's Amy and those terrific kids."

He tilted his head back and looked up at the moon for a long time, then gave a ragged sigh. "We were always honest with each other, you and I. Nothing held back. When I laid eyes on that woman, Ty, it was as though somebody wrenched the ground out from beneath my feet."

While the damning words echoed around him, Harry struggled to face the incomprehensible reality. He hadn't been with Amy Ryan for five minutes before he'd started imagining what it would be like to share his life with her.

He hadn't thought of taking Amy to bed, though God knew that would be the keenest of pleasures. No, he'd pictured her nursing a baby...his baby. He'd seen her running along the white sand on the beach near his house in northern Queensland, with Ashley and Oliver scampering behind, and he'd seen her sitting beside him in the cockpit of his jet.

This was serious.

He touched his friend's headstone as he passed, and started toward the well-lighted parking lot. "If you know what's good for you, Harry," he muttered to himself, "you'll give the lady her money and then stay out of her way."

Harry got behind the wheel of his rented vehicle and started the engine. Nothing must be allowed to happen between him and Amy Ryan, and the reason was simple. To touch her would be to betray a man who would have trusted Harry with his very life.

Three

Amy didn't sleep well that night. She was filled with contradictory feelings; new ones and old ones, affectionate and angry ones. She was furious with Tyler for ever dying in the first place, and with Harry Griffith for thawing out her frozen emotions. She was also experiencing a warmth and a sense of pleasant vulnerability she'd never expected to know again.

After Oliver and Ashley had gone to camp, Amy didn't put on a power suit and go out to network with half a dozen potential clients as she normally would have done. Instead, she wore jeans and a pastel blue sun top and pulled her heavy shoulder-length hair back into a ponytail. She was in the spacious room that had once been Tyler's study, balancing her checkbook and listening with half an ear to a TV talk show, when the telephone rang.

Amy pushed the speaker button. "Hello?"

Harry's smooth, cultured voice filled the room. "Hello, Amy. It's Harry Griffith."

"I know," Amy answered automatically, before she'd had a chance to think about the implications of those two simple words. She laid down her pen and closed the checkbook, feeling vaguely embarrassed. She wanted to say something witty, but of course nothing came to mind; in an hour or a day or a week, when it was too late, some smidgen of clever repartee would come to mind in a flash.

"I enjoyed last night's visit with you and the children," he went on, and Amy leaned back in her chair, just letting that wonderful voice roll over her, like warm ocean water. "Thank you for inviting me, Amy."

Amy closed her eyes, then quickly opened them again. She needed to be on her guard with this man, lest she say or do something really foolish. "Uh... yes...well, you're very welcome, of course." *That was really brilliant, Ryan,* she added to herself.

"I'd like to return the favor, if I might. I've made an appointment to look at a rather unique house over on Vashon Island tomorrow, and I could really use some company—besides the real estate agent, I mean. Would you and Ashley and Oliver care to go out and offer your opinion of the place?"

Amy's heart warmed as she thought how her son and daughter would enjoy such an outing, especially when it meant close contact with Harry. She wasn't exactly averse to the idea herself, though she couldn't quite admit that, even in the privacy of her own soul.

"It would give you and me a chance to discuss that business you mentioned last night." That was the best attempt at setting up a barrier Amy could manage.

Harry sighed. "Yes, there is that. Shall I pick the three of you up tomorrow, then? Around nine?"

A sweet shiver skittered down Amy's spine. "Yes," she heard herself say. But the moment Harry rang off, she wanted to call him back and say she'd changed her mind, she couldn't possibly spend a day on Vashon. She would tell him she had to clean the garage or prune the lilac bushes or something.

Only she had no idea where to reach the charming Mr. Griffith. He hadn't left a number or mentioned the name of a hotel.

Feeling restless, Amy pushed the microphone button on the telephone and thrust herself out of her chair. So much for balancing her checking account; thanks to Harry's call, she wouldn't have been able to subtract two from seven.

Amy paced in front of the natural rock fireplace, wondering where all this unwanted energy had come from. For two years, she'd been concentrating on basic emotional survival. Now, all of the sudden she felt as though she could replaster every wall in that big colonial house without even working up a sweat.

She dialed Debbie's private number at the counseling center.

"I'm going crazy," she blurted out the moment her friend answered.

Debbie laughed. "Amy, I presume? What's happened now? Have you been visited by the ghost of Christmas Weird?"

Amy gave a sigh. "This is serious, Debbie. Harry Griffith just called and invited me to go to Vashon Island with him tomorrow, and I accepted!"

"That *is* terrible," Debbie teased. "Think of it. After only *two years* of mourning, you're actually coming back to life. Quick, head for the nearest closet and hide out until the urge passes!"

Rolling her eyes and twisting the telephone cord around her index finger, Amy replied, "Will you stop with the irony, please? Something very strange is going on here."

Debbie's voice became firm, reasonable. She had become the counselor. "I know a crazy person when I see one, Amy, and believe me, you're completely sane."

"I saw Tyler again last night," Amy insisted. "He was sitting in the backyard swing."

"Your deeper mind is trying to tell you something, Ryan. Pay attention."

"You've been a tremendous help," Amy said with dry annoyance.

Debbie sighed philosophically. "There go my fond hopes of writing a best-selling book, becoming the next self-help guru and appearing on *Oprah.*"

"Debbie."

"Just relax, Amy. That's all you have to do. Stop analyzing everything and just take things one day at a time."

Amy let out a long breath, knowing her friend was right. Which didn't mean for one moment that she'd be able to *apply* the information. "By the way, thanks for sending your cousin Max over last night. My virtue is safe."

Debbie chuckled. "Too safe, methinks. Talk to you later."

Amy said goodbye and hung up. She went into the kitchen and turned on the dishwasher. Almost immediately, water began to seep out from under the door.

"Great," she muttered.

As the rest of the day passed, Amy discovered that her normal tactics for distracting herself weren't working any better than the dishwasher. She had absolutely no desire to contact prospective clients, make follow-up calls or update her files.

At two o'clock, a serviceman came to repair the damage Max had unwittingly done to the dishwasher. Amy watched two soap operas, having no idea who the characters were or what in the world they were talking about. She was relieved when it was finally time to pick the kids up at day camp.

The announcement that Harry had invited the three of them to spend the next day on the island brought whoops of delight from Oliver and a sweet smile from Ashley.

After those reactions, Amy could not have disappointed her children for anything.

That night in bed, she tossed and turned, half hoping Tyler would appear again so she could give him a piece of her mind. Of course, she reasoned, he probably *was* a piece of her mind.

When the first finger of light reached over the mountains visible from Amy's window, Oliver materialized at the foot of her bed. He scrambled onto the mattress and gave a few exuberant leaps.

"Get up, Mom! You've only got four hours to get beautiful before Harry comes to pick us up!"

Amy pulled the covers over her head and groaned. "Oliver, children have been disowned for lesser offenses."

Oliver bounded to the head of the bed and bounced on his knees, simultaneously dragging the blankets back from Amy's face. "This is your big chance, Mom," he argued. "Don't blow it!"

Shoving one hand through her rumpled hair, Amy let out a long sigh. "Trust me, Oliver—while I may appear hopeless to you, I have not quite reached the point of desperation."

The words were no sooner out of her mouth when Tyler's accusation echoed in her mind. *You're not happy.*

The assertion would have been much easier to deal with if it hadn't been fundamentally true. Amy loved her children, and she found her work at least tolerable. She had good health, a nice home and plenty of money.

Those things should have been enough, to her way of thinking, but they weren't. Amy wanted something more.

By the time nine o'clock rolled around, Amy had put on jeans and a navy sweater with red, white and yellow nautical designs. She wore light makeup and a narrow white scarf to hold her hair back from her face.

"Am I presentable?" she whispered to Oliver with a twinkle in her eyes, when the doorbell sounded.

Oliver had already rushed to answer the door, but Ashley examined her mother with a pensive frown and then nodded solemnly. "I suppose you'll do," she said.

When Amy saw Harry standing there on the porch, looking rakishly handsome even in jeans and a white cable-knit sweater, her heart raced the way it did when she was trying to get in step with a revolving door.

His too-blue eyes swept lightly over Amy, but with respect rather than condescension. "G'day," he said.

The children's laughter seemed to startle Harry, though he looked suavely good-natured, as usual.

"You sounded like Crocodile Dundee again," Amy explained with an amused smile. She was grateful to the children for lightening up the situation; if it had been left to her, she probably wouldn't have been able to manage a word. "Come in."

Harry smiled at the kids and rumpled Oliver's hair. Then, as if he hadn't already charmed the eight-year-old right out of her sneakers, he bowed and kissed

Ashley's hand. The effect was oddly continental, despite the child's diminutive size.

Minutes later, after making sure that Oliver and Ashley's seat belts were properly fastened, Harry joined Amy in the front seat.

"You're quite competent at driving on the right-hand side of the road," she remarked, strictly to make conversation, when Harry had backed the van out onto the quiet residential street. An instant later, Amy's cheeks were flooded with color.

Harry's grin could only be described as sweetly wicked. "I've spent considerable time in the States," he responded after a time.

Amy ran the tip of her tongue over dry lips. With Tyler, there had always been so much to talk about, the words had just tumbled from her mouth, but now she felt as though the fate of the western hemisphere hung on every phrase she uttered.

Lamely, she turned to look out the window, all the while riffling through the files in her mind for something witty and sophisticated to say.

"Mom isn't used to dating," Oliver put in from the back, his tones eager and earnest. "You'll have to be patient with her."

Harry chuckled at Amy's groan of mortification, then sent a seismic shock through her system by innocently touching her knee.

"It's all *right*," he assured her in his quiet, elegant, hot-buttered-rum voice. "Why are you so nervous?"

Why, indeed, Amy wondered. Maybe it was because she was really beginning to believe that a ghost had set her up for a blind date!

"Oliver was right on," she said after a few moments of struggling to get her inner balance. "I'm not used to—socializing."

Harry grinned, skillfully shifting the van into a higher gear and keeping to the right of the yellow line on the highway. "Dating," he corrected.

Amy's color flared again, and that only amused him more.

"No wonder Ty was so crazy about you," he observed, keeping his indigo gaze on the traffic.

Foolishly pleased by the compliment, if mystified, Amy did her best to relax.

The lull obviously worried the children; this time it was Ashley who leaned forward to put in her two cents' worth.

"Once Mom went out with this dude who sold real estate," the little girl said sagely. "Rumpel bit his ankle, and the guy threatened to sue."

Amy shook her head and closed her eyes, beyond embarrassment. Then she risked a sidelong glance at Harry. "Rumpel has always been an excellent judge of character," she admitted.

Harry laughed. "All the same, I'll watch my manners when the cat's about."

The thought of Harry Griffith *not* watching his manners made a delicious little thrill tumble through Amy.

Presently they arrived in west Seattle, and Harry took the exit leading to the ferry terminal. He paid the toll and drove onto the enormous white boat with all the savoir faire of a native.

Ashley and Oliver were bouncing in their seats, but Amy made them stay in the van until the boat had been loaded. Their eagerness carried a sweet sting; riding on ferry boats had been something they did with Tyler. He'd taken them from stem to stern and, on one occasion, even into the wheelhouse to meet the captain.

The four of them climbed the metal stairway to the upper deck, Oliver and Harry in the lead, and then walked through the seating area and outside. The wind was crisp and salty and lightly tinged with motor oil.

While Oliver and Ashley ran wildly along the deck, exulting in the sheer freedom of that, Amy leaned against the railing as the heavy boat labored away from shore.

She was only too conscious of Harry standing at her side, mere inches away. He was at once sturdy as a wall and warm as a fire on a wintry afternoon, and Amy was sure she would have sensed his presence even in a pitch-black cellar.

"Have you seen pictures of this place we're going to look at?" she asked, and she sounded squeaky in her effort to keep things light.

Harry shook his head. "No, but the agent described it to me. Sounds like a terrific place."

Amy swallowed. So far, so good. "You'll be renting it, I suppose?"

"Buying," Harry responded. "My company is opening offices in Seattle. I'll be here about six months of the year."

Amy had a peculiar, spiraling sensation in the pit of her stomach. "Oh." She was saved from having to make more of that urbane utterance when Ashley and Oliver returned to collect Harry. They each took a hand, and in moments he was being led away toward the bow.

Wishing she'd had a chance to warn her son and daughter not to promote her like some revolutionary new product about to hit the supermarket shelves, Amy watched the trio stroll away in silence.

When Harry returned from inside, he brought coffee in plastic cups. The kids had a cinnamon roll but, instead of eating it, they were feeding bits and pieces to the gulls.

"They're very beautiful children," he said. The sadness in his tone resonated inside Amy like a musical chord.

"Do you have any kids?" she asked.

Harry sighed and stared at the receding shoreline and city. "I had a stepdaughter once. She died with her mother in a plane crash."

Amy winced inwardly. Losing her husband had been torment enough. To lose Tyler *and* one or both of her children would have been unbearable. "I'm so sorry," she said.

Harry's smile was dazzling, like sunlight mixing with sparkling water early on a summer morning. "It's been a long time ago now, love. Don't let it trouble you."

"Have you any other family?" Amy wasn't to be so easily turned aside.

"My mother," Harry answered with a grin. "She's a Hun, but I love her."

Amy laughed.

"What about your mother?" Harry asked. "Is she beautiful, like you and Ashley?"

Once again, he'd used an invisible emotional cord to trip her. She tightened her grip on the railing and felt her smile float away on the tide. "She died when I was four. I don't remember her."

It seemed perfectly natural for Harry to put his arm around her shoulders. Amy felt comforted by the gesture. "You've had a great deal of loss in your life," he said gently. "What about your father? Do you have one of those?"

Amy nodded, squaring her shoulders and working up a smile. "He's a doctor, always busy. I don't see him much."

"Do I detect a note of loneliness?" Harry asked, letting his arm fall back to his side again. He seemed to know intuitively when to touch and when not to, when to talk and when to keep silent.

A denial rushed into Amy's throat. Lonely? She had her beautiful children, her friends, her job. "Of course I'm not—"

"Lonely," Harry finished for her, arching one eyebrow.

Amy sighed. "Okay," she confessed, "so sometimes I feel a little isolated. Doesn't everybody have moments like that?"

The wind lifted a tendril of Harry's perfect hair. "Some people have *decades* like that," he replied, leaning against the railing now, bracing himself easily with both forearms. "Even lifetimes, poor souls."

A brief boldness possessed Amy. "What about you?" she asked. But an instant later she wished she could call the question back because it made her look like such a naive fool. Of course a rich, handsome, sophisticated man like Harry Griffith would never be subject to such a forlorn emotion as loneliness.

"There were days—nights, more particularly— when I honestly thought I'd die of it," he confessed, looking Amy directly in the eye.

She didn't think Harry was lying, and yet she couldn't imagine him in such a state. He was obviously a jet-setter, and women were probably willing to wrestle in the mud for the chance to be with him.

He smiled. "I can see by your expression that you're skeptical, Mrs. Ryan," he teased.

Harry Griffith was as suave and handsome as Cary Grant had been in his youth, and Amy could well imagine him as an elegant jewel thief. "Well, it's just—"

He cupped her chin lightly in his hand and stroked her lips with the pad of his thumb, making them want to be kissed. "Being surrounded by people doesn't make a person immune to emotional pain, Amy."

She could feel herself being pulled toward him by some unseen inner force. Harry's mouth was descending toward hers, at just the right angle for the kiss she suddenly craved, but Oliver prevented full contact.

"Mom?" he shouted, tugging at her sleeve. "Hey, Mom? When we get to the island, is it okay if I go swimming?"

Amy pulled back from Harry. Her frustration knew no bounds, and yet she spoke to her son in reasonable tones. "Puget Sound is too cold for swimming, Oliver," she said. "You know that."

Harry reached out to rumple the boy's hair affectionately, an understanding grin curving his lips, and Amy liked the Australian all the more for being so perceptive.

Soon they reached the island, driving ashore in Harry's van. He brought a small notebook from the catch-all space between the front seats and consulted some hastily scrawled directions with a thoughtful frown. After that, he seemed to know exactly what he was doing.

Within fifteen minutes, they pulled up beside the kind of place northwest artists loved to sketch. It was a lighthouse, built of white stone, with a long house stretching out in one direction, its many windows sparkling in the sunshine. On the other side was a fenced courtyard, complete with rose bushes, stone benches and a marble fountain.

Amy drew in her breath. "Harry, it's wonderful," she said.

A perfect gentleman, Harry had come around to her side of the van. Perhaps it was an accident, and perhaps it wasn't, that her midsection slid the length of his when he lifted her down. "Then I'll have no choice but to sign the papers," he said, his mouth very close to hers again.

Oliver and Ashley were sizing up the lighthouse, heads tilted back, eyes wide.

"I'll bet you can see all the way to China from up there!" Oliver crowed.

Ashley gave him a little shove. "Don't be a dummy. You'll only be able to see Seattle."

An expensive white car came up the cobbled driveway and stopped behind Harry's van. A tall, artfully made-up woman with champagne-blond hair got out. She was wearing a trim suit in the palest pink, with a classic white blouse, and Amy suddenly felt downright provincial in her jeans and nautical sweater.

"Mr. Griffith?" the woman asked, smiling and extending her hand. As she drew closer, Amy let out her breath. The real estate agent was strikingly attractive, but she was also old enough to be Harry's mother. "I'm Eva Caldwell," she added. Her bright eyes swept over Amy and the children. "And this must be your family."

Harry only grinned, but Amy was discomfited by the suggestion. No matter what her subconscious mind had to say through very convincing images of her late husband, Harry Griffith was not the sort of man to want a ready-made family. He was the type that married a beautiful heiress and honeymooned on a private yacht somewhere among the Greek Islands.

"We're just his friends," Ashley piped up.

"Very good friends," Harry confirmed, giving Ashley's shoulder a little squeeze.

Mrs. Caldwell jingled a set of keys, her smile at once warm and professional, and started toward the double mahogany doors leading into the addition. "The lighthouse, of course, was the original structure. The other rooms were built around the turn of the century..."

The inside of the place was as intriguing as the outside. On the lower level was a living room with beamed ceilings. It stretched the width of the house, and the wall of windows gave a startling view of the water. The floors were pegged wood, and there was a massive fireplace at one end, with brass andirons on the hearth and built-in bookshelves on both sides.

On the far side of the room was an arched doorway leading to a hallway. There were four bedrooms beyond that, the master suite with a natural rock fireplace of its own, and up a short flight of stairs was a large loft, offering the same view of Puget Sound as the living room.

There was a door leading from the loft into the lighthouse itself. The kids rushed up the spiral staircase ahead of Mrs. Caldwell and Harry and Amy, in their excitement to see China or, failing that, Seattle.

"A place like this ought to come with a ghost, by all rights," Harry remarked.

If he'd tossed Amy a leaky plastic bag filled with ice, Harry couldn't have startled her more. She stopped on the stairs and stared at him, feeling the color drain from her face, wondering if he somehow knew she was seeing things and wanted to make fun of her.

"Amy?" He stopped, letting Mrs. Caldwell go on ahead. She was still talking, unaware that her prospect was lagging behind. "What's the matter?"

The calm reason of his tone and manner made Amy feel silly. Of *course* he didn't have an inkling that she'd seen Tyler, and as brief as their acquaintance had been, she knew Harry was above needling another person in such a callous way.

"Nothing's the matter," she answered finally. Her smile felt wobbly on her lips.

Harry frowned, but then he reached out to her, as naturally as if they'd always been together. Just as naturally Amy took his hand and they climbed the rest of the way together.

In the top of the old but well-maintained tower was a surprisingly modern electric light.

"The lighthouse is still used when the weather gets particularly nasty," Mrs. Caldwell explained.

"I can see Seattle!" Oliver whooped from the other side of the little causeway that surrounded the massive, many-faceted lamp.

"He's apparently given up on China," Harry whispered with a slight smile and a lift of one eyebrow.

Amy felt just the way she once had as a kid at summer camp, when she'd fallen off a horse and knocked the wind out of her lungs. Remarkable that just a hint of a smile could have such an effect.

"Spend as much time looking as you'd like," Mrs. Caldwell said, holding out a single key to Harry. She gave him brief directions to her office, which was near the ferry terminal, and asked him to stop by before he left.

When Ashley and Oliver raced back downstairs to check out the yard, Harry and Amy remained where they were.

Amy read the sober expression in Harry's eyes as consternation. He frowned again, as though she'd said something he was forced to disagree with, and then pulled her close and kissed her.

The gentle, skilled prodding of his tongue made her open to him, and she gave an involuntary moan, surrendering even before the skirmish had begun.

Harry held her hips in his hands, pressing her lightly against him. He nibbled at her lower lip and tasted the corners of her mouth, and still the gentle conquering went on.

Finally, though, Harry thrust himself back from her. He was breathing hard as though he'd just barely managed to escape a powerful undercurrent.

"I'm sorry," he said, and although Amy knew he had to be talking to her, it was almost as though he were addressing someone else.

An apology was probably the last thing Amy had wanted to hear. She was still responding, body and spirit, to the kiss, still reeling from the way she'd wanted him. She cleared her throat delicately and led the way downstairs without a word, using the time with her back to Harry to regain her composure.

"What do you think of the place?" he asked sometime later, when the four of them had built a driftwood fire on the beach and brought a cooler and a picnic basket from the van.

"It's wonderful," Amy answered, feeling her cheeks go warm as an echo of Harry's thorough kiss tingled on her mouth.

Harry surveyed the beautiful lighthouse pensively as he roasted a marshmallow over the fire. "It's big," he countered.

Ashley and Oliver were running wildly up and down the beach, their cheeks bright with color, their laughter ringing in the salty air. Amy couldn't remember the last time she'd seen them enjoy an outing so much.

She put a marshmallow on another stick and watched it turn crisp and bubbly over the flames. "I imagine you can see the ferry lights from the living room at night," she said a little dreamily.

Harry ate the sticky marshmallow he'd just roasted, and Amy imagined that his lips would taste of it if he kissed her again. For a long moment she honestly thought he was about to, but then he started gathering the debris from their picnic on the beach.

Amy helped, and by the time they reached the real estate office, Ashley and Oliver were already asleep in the back of the van and a light rain was falling.

Waiting in the van, watching the windshield wipers whip back and forth over the glass, Amy felt sad, as though she were leaving the one place where she really belonged.

Four

—

Harry Griffith was not a fanciful man. He dealt in stark realities and played for very high stakes, and he hadn't done an impetuous thing since he was seven years old.

For all of that, he signed the papers to buy the lighthouse when he'd only meant to drop off the keys. He couldn't stop imagining Amy in the massive living room, reflected firelight glittering in her golden brown hair. Or in his bed, her trim yet lush body all soft and warm and welcoming.

If that wasn't enough to haunt a man for days, the mingled sounds of the children's laughter and the tide whispering against the shore were still echoing in his mind.

"I'm sure you'll be very happy on the island," Mrs. Caldwell said.

"I'm sure I will," Harry agreed, but he wasn't thinking about the view or the clams and oysters he could gather. He was obsessed with Amy Ryan, had been practically from the moment he'd met her.

Mrs. Caldwell smiled. "Do let me know if there's anything else I can do," she said. She and Harry shook hands, and then he turned and sprinted out into the rain to rejoin Amy and the children in the van.

Amy looked every bit as nervous and unsettled as he felt.

"I bought the house," he announced, the moment he'd closed the door and put the key into the ignition. Again Harry had taken himself by surprise; he'd definitely decided, only moments before, that he wouldn't mention the purchase to Amy until they knew each other better.

She seemed a bit bewildered, but there might have been just a glimmer of pleasure in those wonderful hazel eyes, too. Harry, who was usually such a good judge of people, couldn't be certain.

"You won't find a more charming place anywhere in the country," she said after a few moments of silence.

Harry glanced back over one shoulder at the sleeping children. "Do you think they'll wake up for dinner? We could stop somewhere on the other side..."

Amy shook her head. "Thank you for offering," she said softly, "but I think it would be best if I took them straight home. They've had a pretty full day as it is, and any more excitement would probably put them on overload."

Harry felt another new emotion: chagrin. Maybe he'd offended Amy by kissing her earlier that day in the lighthouse, made her wonder what kind of friend he could have been to Tyler. God help him, Harry had known better than to do what he did, but he hadn't been able to stop himself.

His vocal cords seemed to be on automatic pilot, yet another unfamiliar experience. All his adult life, except for those few whiskey-sodden days after he'd learned of Tyler's death, Harry had been in complete control of all his faculties. Now, suddenly, nothing seemed to follow its usual order.

"Tomorrow night, then?" he asked, before he could measure the words in his mind.

She smiled at him with a certain sweet weariness that made him want to give her comfort and pleasure. "Oliver and Ashley will be spending the day with Tyler's folks," she said, and he wondered if she expected him to withdraw the invitation because of that.

"But you won't be?"

Amy shrugged one strong but delicate shoulder. "I'd be welcome if I wanted to go. But I think both the kids and Mom and Dad Ryan need time to interact without me hovering around somewhere."

Harry rode the crest of foolhardy bravado that seemed to be carrying him along. "Fine. Then you'll be free to have dinner with me."

He sensed that she was carrying on some inner struggle, he was aware of it all the while he paid the toll and drove onto the Seattle-bound ferry, and the fear that she would refuse was as keenly painful as a nerve exposed to cold air.

"I'd like that," she finally said, her voice soft and cautious.

With some effort, Harry held back a shout of gleeful triumph—the sensation was rather like scoring the winning goal in a soccer match—and managed what he hoped was an easy, man-of-the-world smile.

"So would I," he agreed. "So would I."

Charlotte Ryan's voice echoed off the walls of Amy's closet as she plundered the contents for something suitable for that night's heavy date. Small, with sleek dark hair and inquisitive brown eyes, Charlotte was one of Amy's closest friends. Tyler had always referred to her as "my favorite sister," subsequently making light of the fact that she was his *only* sister.

She came out carrying a sophisticated silver-lamé sheath with a gracefully draped neckline.

"This is perfect," Charlotte announced. "Which isn't to say you couldn't give a lot of that stuff in there to the Salvation Army and start fresh with a whole new wardrobe."

The glittery dress was expensive, and one of the few garments in Amy's closet that wasn't a holdover from the fairy-tale time before Tyler's death. She'd bought it a few months ago for a banquet honoring her father and hadn't worn it since.

"Maybe it's too fancy," Amy fretted. "For all I know, we're going to a waterfront stand for fish and chips."

"With Harry Griffith?" Charlotte countered, laying the dress carefully on the bed. "Not on your life, Amy. The man is class personified. Mark my words, he'll be wearing a tux and holding flowers when he rings the doorbell."

Amy's heart rate quickened at the romantic thought, and she was instantly ashamed of the reaction. Tyler would be so hurt if he knew the depths of the attraction she was feeling for Harry Griffith.

Immediately her mind presented a counterpoint to its own suggestion, reminding her that it had been Tyler who'd told her she was supposed to marry Harry, even bear his children.

It was all too confusing.

Charlotte was waving one hand back and forth in front of Amy's face. "Yo, sister dear," she teased. "Are you in there?"

Amy busied herself finding panty hose in her bureau drawer. "How long is it supposed to take to get over... well, to get over becoming a widow?"

Her sister-in-law was silent for a long moment. Then she laid a gentle hand on Amy's shoulder. "I don't think there are any written rules about that. But I do know Ty wouldn't want you to spend the rest of your life grieving for him, Amy."

Tears burned in Amy's eyes and thickened in her throat. "I loved him so much."

Charlotte came around to face Amy and give her a quick hug. "I know," she said. "But, Amy, he's gone, and you're still young..."

"It's Ty's fault that I'm so hesitant to get into another relationship, you know," Amy sniffled. "Marriage to him was so wonderful, nothing else could possibly be expected to equal it."

Charlotte's eyes widened, and she chuckled. "That's the damnedest reason for staying single I've ever heard! You're scared of finding another husband because you were *too happy* the first time?"

"I know it sounds crazy," Amy insisted, pushing her bureau drawer shut with a thump, "but Tyler Ryan would be a very hard act to follow."

"Don't expect me to argue," Charlotte said, her eyes moist with emotion. "I loved my brother a lot. He was an original. But you can't just hide out in your career for the next forty years, waiting to join him in the great beyond. You've got to get out there and *live.*"

"Who says?" Amy asked, but she knew Charlotte was right. Life was a precious gift; to waste it was the unpardonable sin.

Charlotte gave Amy a little shove toward the bathroom. "Get in there and take a long, luxurious bubble bath. I'll drop the kids off at Mom and Dad's."

Amy sniffled one last time. "Thanks," she said hoarsely, giving her sister-in-law another hug.

Taking Charlotte's advice to heart, Amy filled the tub in her private bathroom, adding generous amounts of the expensive bubble bath her father had given her for Christmas the year before. She pinned up her thick hair and hung her long white terry-cloth robe on the hook on the inside of the door.

Amy stripped and sank gratefully into the warm, soapy water.

"Charlotte's right," Tyler announced suddenly, so startling Amy that she barely kept herself from screaming. "Harry is a classy guy."

Tyler, dressed in a vaguely familiar blue-and-white warm-up suit, stood with one foot resting on the toilet seat, elbow propped on his knee, chin resting in his palm.

"You might have knocked or something!" Amy hissed, when she was finally able to speak.

"Knocked?" Ty looked downright offended. "We were married once, in case you've forgotten."

Amy sighed. "Of course I haven't forgotten. And what do you mean, we *were* married?"

Tyler shrugged and pretended a sober interest in the composition of the shower curtain. "You know. I'm here, you're there. And you've got a lot of time left on your hitch, Spud, so you'd better get your act together."

She started to rise out of the water, felt self-conscious, and decided to keep herself cloaked in the piles of iridescent bubbles. Then she narrowed her eyes. "Are you saying that you plan to go on to wherever you're going without me?" she demanded.

"The bargain was 'till death do us part,' darlin'. And don't look now, but death done parted us."

Amy felt a wrenching sensation deep within her, a tearing away that seemed decidedly permanent. "You've met someone!"

Tyler grinned. "It doesn't work that way on this side, Spud. And even if there were some kind of celestial dating service, I have too much work to do to take time out for a relationship."

He looked so real, as if she could reach out and touch him and he'd feel solid under her hand. She made no effort to do that, however, because the memory of the way he'd pulled back from her the other time was still fresh in her mind.

Amy leaned back against the blue plastic bathtub pillow and closed her eyes. "I'm hallucinating," she said. "When I open my eyes, you will be gone."

But when she looked again, Tyler was still standing there. "Are you through?" he asked a little impatiently. "I told you before, Amy... my energy is limited and I don't have time to play 'is he or isn't he?'"

Amy's mouth dropped open, and she closed it again.

"Harry's taking you to the Stardust Ballroom," Tyler went on. "He's very attracted to you, but he's also having some conflicts. It bothers him that you were my wife."

Amy waited, in shock.

"You've got to reassure Harry somehow, before he comes up with some excuse to go back to Australia and stay there. I'm counting on you, Amy."

There was an urgency in Tyler's tone that troubled Amy, but she had her hands full just trying to cope with *seeing* him. She blinked, that was all, just blinked, and when she looked again her husband's ghost was gone.

Relaxing in the bathtub was out of the question, of course. In fact, Amy wasn't sure she shouldn't call 911 and have herself trundled off to the pot-holder-weaving department of the nearest hospital.

She jumped up, grabbed her robe and wrapped it around herself without taking the time to dry off. The thing to do was call Harry and beg off from their dinner date. She could claim illness, since there seemed to be every possibility she was losing her mind!

The trouble was, Amy still didn't have Harry's number, nor did she know where he was staying.

But the Ryans might. Surely Harry had contacted Tyler's parents, since he'd lived in their home as an exchange student for six months, back in high school...

Amy was about to dive for the telephone when her eyes fell on the spray of white lilacs lying on her pillow. Their lovely scent seemed to fill the room.

The blossoms were Tyler's special signature. In the old days, before the great and all-encompassing grief that had practically swallowed Amy's very soul, he'd often cut a bouquet in the back yard and presented them to her in just this way.

Her eyes stung. "Oh, Tyler," she whispered.

Since she knew she'd obsess if she stayed home, Amy went ahead with the preparations for her dinner date. She applied makeup, put on the shimmery dress and did her hair up in a loose bun at the back of her head. A few tendrils of sun-streaked blond hair were left to dangle against her cheeks and neck.

She was in the den, pacing, when the doorbell rang.

Opening the door, Amy found Harry waiting on the step. He was wearing a tux, just as Charlotte had predicted, and he looked like an advertisement for some exclusive European wristwatch. In one hand he carried a delicate bouquet of exotic pink-and-white blossoms.

His blue eyes darkened slightly as he looked at Amy, then he smiled and held out the flowers, along with a long white envelope.

"You must surely be the most beautiful woman in the whole of the western hemisphere," he said, his voice a low, rumbling caress that struck sparks in some very tender parts of Amy's anatomy.

"Come in," Amy said, sounding a lot more composed than she felt, stepping back to admit him. She admired the velvety pastel lilies for a moment, then turned the envelope over, as if its back might reveal its contents.

"Your dividend on Tyler's investment in the opal mines," Harry explained, his voice a bit gruff. He cleared his throat, but it didn't seem to help much. "Obviously I forgot to give it to you yesterday."

Amy hesitated.

"Open it," Harry prompted, closing the door.

She tore off the end of the envelope and slipped the check out. As financially secure as Amy was, the amount still came as a pleasant shock. It was enough to buy a decent house outright.

"Tyler must have made a very large investment," she mused.

"Actually, he put up the accumulated birthday money from his grandmother," Harry explained.

Amy went into the den and put the check between the pages of her personal journal. Harry stood with his back to her, in front of the stone fireplace, looking at the row of pictures on the mantel.

When he turned to face Amy, the thought flew into her mind that she could probably achieve some distance between them by telling Harry she'd seen Tyler on three different occasions. Odd that she was more frightened of this living, breathing man than of a dead one.

"Shall we?" he said, offering his arm.

Amy couldn't bring herself to mention her hallucinations. "Just let me put these lilies in water," she said hastily, turning to hurry into the kitchen for a shallow bowl.

Floating in that fiery crystal, the flowers were so beautiful that they made Amy's throat swell.

There was a white limousine, complete with driver, waiting at the curb. Harry helped Amy into the backseat, which was upholstered in suede of a smoky blue, and climbed in beside her.

"I forgot to thank you for the dividend check," Amy said, feeling awkward and shy again. She couldn't help remembering the kiss she and Harry had shared the day before; just the thought of it made her go all warm and achy inside.

Harry gave an elegant shrug. "It's rightfully yours," he said. Then he reached out and lightly entwined his finger in one of the wisps of hair bobbing against Amy's cheek. "Such a bewitching creature," he added, as if musing to himself rather than speaking to her. "If a being as lovely and magical as you can exist, then surely there must be unicorns somewhere in this world as well."

Amy felt dizzy. "That's some line," she said, after a few moments of being totally inarticulate.

He smiled. "Oh, it's not a line," he assured her suavely. "I meant every word."

Amy believed him, although she knew she should have had her head examined for it. Next, he'd be telling her that no other woman had ever understood him the way she did, and asking her to come to his hotel room to view his etchings.

She ran the tip of her tongue over her lips. The gesture was quick, over in a second, but Harry followed it with his eyes, and it seemed that time stopped for a little while. That she and Harry were alone in the universe.

For all of the thrumming attraction she'd felt ever since she'd met this man, their second kiss startled her completely.

Harry tasted her lips expertly, as though they were flavored with the finest wine, sending little shocks reverberating throughout her system. He might have been kissing her much more intimately, given the responses the contact wrought in her, and when his hand cupped her breast, she gave a whispered moan and tilted her head back.

He sampled her neck, the tender hollows beneath her ear, the pulse point at the base of her throat.

Harry apparently remembered the driver, even if Amy, to her vast chagrin, did not. He drew back from her, smiled in a way that made her heart and throat collide at breakneck speed, and caressed her cheek with the side of his thumb.

He didn't have to say he wanted to make love to Amy; his eyes told her clearly enough.

Minutes later, when the limousine was purring at a downtown curb, the driver came back to open the door. Amy was grateful for the cool breeze that met her as she stepped out onto the sidewalk.

She was also enormously relieved, because the restaurant was not the Stardust Ballroom, as Tyler had predicted. That made things a little less spooky.

The place was shadowy and elegant, with candles flickering in the centers of the tables, and the atmosphere was intimate. Amy hoped the dimness would hide her bright eyes and glowing cheeks—it wouldn't do for Harry to guess how thoroughly he'd aroused her.

Amy had seafood salad and Harry had a steak, and they both drank a dry, velvety wine. When the meal was over, they danced.

For all that there were other couples around, the experience was another alarmingly intimate one for Amy. The way Harry held her close was in no way inappropriate, but the scent and substance of him excited her in a way nothing in her life had prepared her for. Her breasts and thighs were cushioned against the granite lines of his frame, and Amy's body was responding as though she were naked beneath him, in a private place.

He had guessed what was happening, evidently, for a half smile curved his lips. He gave no quarter.

His lips moved, warm, against her temple. "There's no going back now, love," he warned in a ragged whisper. "It's going to happen—tonight, tomorrow, next week."

Amy knew Harry was right, but as much as she wanted him, the idea of such total surrender terrified her.

He traced her mouth with the tip of one index finger. "So beautiful," he said.

"C-could we sit down, please?"

Harry led her back to their table and seated her with as much grace as if she'd been a princess.

She couldn't meet his eyes, and her cheeks felt as hot as the tip of the candle's flame. After all, she'd practically come apart in the man's arms, and all because of the way he'd been holding her.

Harry reached out to curve his finger under her chin. "We have time, Amy," he reminded her.

Amy was relieved when he didn't ask her to dance again, though. She wasn't sure how much intimate contact she could take without making an absolute fool of herself.

They had Irish coffee and then left the restaurant.

"I think I have a headache coming on," Amy lied, once they were settled in the limousine again. Inside, she was still quivering from the tempestuous desire he'd awakened in her.

Harry grinned. "We can't just go off and leave the driver, now can we?" he teased.

Amy glanced nervously toward the front. There was no sign of the chauffeur. "Maybe I could just take a cab..."

But Harry shook his head before she'd even finished the suggestion. "When I take a lady out," he said in his rich accent, "I always take her home again. Come here, Amy."

She was overwhelmingly conscious of Harry's after-shave, the softness of the suede seats, the gentle command in his dark blue eyes. She tried to think of Tyler and, to her utter frustration, found that she couldn't remember what he'd looked like. Although she would have testified in a court of law that she hadn't moved, Amy suddenly found herself in Harry's arms again.

He kissed her, that was all, and yet Amy felt herself melting like warm wax. For the first time ever, she actually wanted a man other than Tyler, and her emotions were as tangled as a string of garage-sale Christmas tree lights.

The tinted windows of the limousine provided a high degree of privacy; the fact that the driver could return at any moment lent the situation a sense of breathless urgency.

She heard the electric locks on the limousine's doors click into place, and that made her eyes go wide.

He did nothing more than kiss and hold her, and yet Amy felt like some succulent dessert. Everything seemed to be happening in slow motion, and Amy was helpless to stop the tide of fate. She was abashed to realize that, if Harry suggested heading straight for his hotel room, she would have agreed.

Suddenly, though, the locks clicked again, and Harry was sitting a respectable distance from her, looking as unruffled as if he'd just stepped from his barber's chair.

Amy, on the contrary, was in a state of blissful shock.

The driver got back into the car, and Amy heard Harry give him a familiar address—her own. The only emotion that exceeded her relief was her disappointment.

On the porch, Harry bent forward to kiss her lightly on the tip of her nose. "You were too delectable to resist," he told her. "I'll try to mind my manners a little better next time."

Amy's senses were still rioting, and she rocked slightly on her heels, so that Harry clasped her elbows to steady her. "You could come in and have coffee," she said, and then she bit her lip. She'd had virtually no experience at being a vamp, since she'd never been with another man besides Tyler.

His smile was sexy enough to be lethal, though there was an element of sadness in it, too. "If I came in tonight, Amy,'' he said, ''I'm afraid I would want much more than coffee. And neither of us is ready.''

With that, Harry kissed her on the forehead—it was a purely innocuous contact that left Amy feeling hollow—and walked away.

She had the presence of mind to turn the lock and put the chain on the door after he was gone, but just barely. She gave a little hiccuping sob when Rumpel appeared and wrapped her sleek, silky body around her ankles.

''Reowww,'' she said companionably.

In need of comfort, Amy scooped the small animal into her arms and hurried up the stairs.

All the while she was taking off her dress and washing her face and putting on cotton pajamas, Amy cried. She had turned some kind of emotional corner, and she knew there would be no going back.

Tyler's mother awakened her with a phone call at ten-thirty the next morning.

''Hello, Amy,'' Louise Ryan said warmly. ''I'm calling to ask a very big favor.''

Amy was only half-awake, and rummy from a night of alternate crying and soul-searching. ''A favor?''

''John and I are leaving for Kansas, the first of next week . . . his side of the family is having a big reunion. We hadn't planned on going, but at the last minute we decided to live a little. And, well, we'd like to take Oliver and Ashley along on the trip, if you don't mind.''

The breathless hope in her mother-in-law's voice brought a tender smile to Amy's mouth.

"Of course they can go, Louise," she said, marveling even as the words left her mouth.

The next few minutes were taken up with the making of plans; John and Louise planned to drive back to the midwest in their motor home, and they wanted to pick the kids up early Monday morning.

"Oliver tells me you've been seeing Harry Griffith," Louise said, when everything had been decided.

Just remembering last night's interlude in the limousine made color flow into Amy's cheeks, but she managed to make her voice sound normal. "I'm not *seeing* him, actually," she hedged. *You are, though,* challenged a voice in her mind. *And admit it, you'd like to do a lot more than that.*

"Harry is a wonderful young man," Louise said brightly.

"Yes," Amy agreed, keeping her tone strictly noncommittal. Despite the fact that she'd behaved like a teenager in the backseat of a Chevy the night before, she had a lot of reservations where Harry Griffith was concerned.

Amy swallowed, winding her finger in the telephone cord. She should tell Louise she'd been seeing Tyler, she knew that, but the risk was just too great. She depended on John and Louise Ryan—for all practical intents and purposes, they were the only family she had—and she didn't want them to think she was having a nervous breakdown or something.

"We'll bring the children home later this morning," Louise went on, apparently failing to notice the long lull on Amy's end of the conversation. "And thank you, dear, for letting us take them on the trip with us."

Amy said something ordinary, something she couldn't remember later, added a warm farewell and hung up. After she'd brushed her teeth and washed her face and generally made herself presentable, she went downstairs in shorts and a T-shirt to let Rumpel out.

She was having a much-needed cup of coffee when the doorbell rang, and when she reached the entryway, she found Harry standing on the step. He was wearing jeans and a sweatshirt, and yet he managed to look as elegantly rakish as an old-time riverboat gambler.

"G'day," he said, leaning one shoulder against the doorjamb. "Is that offer of coffee still open?"

Amy hadn't prepared herself, mentally or otherwise, for an encounter with Harry, and she was caught off guard. She blushed, nodded, and stepped back.

"You know," Harry said with a grin, "it's perfectly charming, the way you do that."

"Do what?" Amy challenged. For some reason she couldn't have put a name to, she needed to contradict him.

"Color up like a naked virgin when the bathhouse wall has just collapsed," he answered. "Are the children about?"

Amy led the way into the kitchen. "No," she answered, grateful that her response only called for simple words. "They're with the Ryans, making plans for a trip."

Harry turned her when she reached for the cupboard where the mugs were stored, and she was trapped between his hard torso and the counter. He traced her mouth with the tip of one index finger. "Excellent," he said. "That leaves you with no rational excuse for refusing to fly to Australia with me tomorrow."

Five

Amy had every rational reason to refuse Harry's invitation to visit Australia with him. She *must* have rational reasons, she thought. It was just that she couldn't summon up a single one on such short notice.

Harry smiled his slow, knee-melting smile, only too aware, evidently, of her dilemma, then arched one eyebrow as if prompting her to produce a suitable answer.

"I don't have a visa for Australia," she finally said, flustered.

Harry outlined the edge of her jaw with a fingertip, sending fire racing through her system. "No worries, love," he said, his voice husky and low. "I can take care of that with a single telephone call."

Amy was trapped and she liked it, and the fact incensed her. "I can't just go flying off to another hemisphere with a man I hardly know!" she pointed out irritably.

He was so close, so solid, so warm. So male. "Ah," he said wisely, "but you *want* to know me quite well, don't you, Amy?"

Coming from any other man, the question would have sounded insufferably arrogant. From Harry, it was the unvarnished, pitiless truth.

"Yes," she confessed weakly, before she could stop herself.

Harry touched his lips to hers, with the lightest brushing motion, and a fiery shiver exploded in the core of her being, flinging rays of sweet heat into all her extremities. In fact, it was a wonder to Amy that her hair didn't crackle.

"Yes," he agreed with a sigh.

They just stood there like that, for an eternity, it seemed to Amy, and then he kissed her forehead.

"I think I'd better go now," he said reluctantly. He laid a finger to her nose. "Pack for a warm climate, love, and bring something for a glamorous occasion."

Amy didn't ask how he'd know when to pick her up. There was something mystical about the whole thing, something preordained. When it was time to leave, Harry would simply be there.

After he was gone, Amy went out into the backyard and stood by the tire swing.

"Tyler!" she demanded in an anxious, self-conscious whisper. "Where are you? I need to talk to you right now!"

There was no answer but for a breeze that ruffled the bushes burgeoning with white lilacs and carried their scent to Amy like a gift.

"This is important!" she pressed, feeling desperate. She knew what was going to happen if she went to Australia with Harry Griffith, and she was terrified. After all, she'd never been intimate with another man, before Tyler or after, and she felt as shy as a virgin.

"What's that, dear?" inquired a pleasant female voice.

Amy looked up to see Mrs. Ingallstadt, her neighbor, peering at her over the fence. The older woman was wearing a gardening hat and wielding clipping shears.

"I was just—" Amy paused to clear her throat and to work up a smile. "I was just thinking out loud, Mrs. Ingallstadt. How are you?"

"Well, my arthritis is going to be the death of me one of these days, and my gall bladder is acting up again, but otherwise I'm pretty chipper. Tell me, dear, how are you?"

Well, Amy thought, *I'm seeing things and I think I'm actually going to get on an airplane and fly away to another continent with a virtual stranger. Other than that, Mrs. Ingallstadt, I'm just fine.*

"I've been keeping busy." Recalling Mrs. Ingallstadt's fondness for white lilacs, and how Tyler had occasionally charmed the old woman with a bouquet,

Amy walked over to one lacy bush and broke off several blossom-laden boughs. Without saying any more, she handed the flowers over the fence to her friend and neighbor.

Mrs. Ingallstadt beamed with pleasure, and Amy realized, with some chagrin, that she'd hardly exchanged a word with the woman in six full months. After Tyler's death, Mrs. Ingallstadt had been wonderful to Amy, and to Ashley and Oliver as well. She'd made meals, baby-sat and listened patiently when Amy was overwhelmed with grief. That first dreadful Christmas, when it seemed there would never again be reason to celebrate, the thoughtful neighbor had come into Amy's kitchen, pushed up her sleeves and proceeded to bake sugar cookies with the children.

"I'll just take these right inside and put them in water," Mrs Ingallstadt said happily. "I don't know why I haven't planted a few lilac bushes of my own. My husband was allergic to them, you know, but Walter's been dead these twenty years and I don't reckon anything could make him sneeze now."

Amy's grin was probably a little on the grim side. *Don't count on it,* she thought.

Later that day, when she'd vacuumed the upstairs hallway and gone through her closet four times, all the while insisting to herself that she *would not* do anything so impetuous as fly to Australia with Harry Griffith, Amy got her suitcases from the guest-room closet and laid them on her bed. Open.

Even then, she told herself she only meant to pack things for Ashley and Oliver to take to Kansas.

Still, when Louise brought the kids home from Mercer Island in her shiny silver Mercedes, Amy had filled the luggage with her own best summer clothes.

She and Louise did the kids' things together. Louise Ryan was an attractive woman, tanned and obviously prosperous, and she was intelligent.

"How was your evening with Harry Griffith?" she asked, snapping the catches on Ashley's suitcase into place.

Color surged into Amy's face, and she didn't quite manage to meet her mother-in-law's gaze. She couldn't help wondering what Louise would think if she knew her son's widow was about to do something completely reckless and wanton.

"I like him," Amy finally replied. She was sure a greater understatement had never been uttered.

Louise smiled, her Tyler-brown eyes laughing. Her hair was a rich auburn color, frosted with silvery gray, and she claimed she was covered in freckles from head to foot. "A woman doesn't simply 'like' a man like our Harry," she said confidently, her gaze steady as she regarded Amy. "She either finds him totally intolerable or can't keep her hands off him."

Guess which category I fall into, Amy thought ruefully, her face going warm again. "I guess Tyler liked him a lot," she hedged, picking up Ashley's suitcase and lugging it to the doorway. Its weight didn't justify the effort, however, and she had a feeling Louise knew that.

"Tyler thought the world of Harry Griffith. So do the rest of us."

As understanding and progressive a woman as Louise was, Amy still couldn't make herself confide that she was wildly attracted to Harry. The thought reverberated inside her mind, however, like the silent toll of some mystic bell. "He's a nice man," was all she said.

After Ashley and Oliver had left the house with their grandmother, bag and baggage, Amy felt as insubstantial as an echo, bouncing aimlessly between one empty room and another. Finally, she went to the phone and dialed Debbie's home number, knowing she'd get an answering machine because her friend would be at the clinic.

"Hi," Amy said with a stilted effort at normalcy, "this is Amy. I just wanted to let you know that, well, I've completely lost my mind. Harry Griffith invited me to fly to Australia in his private jet, and God help me I'm going to do it." Color flooded her cheeks, even though she was talking to a whirring mechanism and not another human being. "Actually, *do it* isn't precisely the phrasing I was looking for, although I'm a grown woman and responsible person and if I want to do—anything—oh, never mind!" Amy forcibly stopped herself from rambling, drew a deep breath and let it out again. "I'm going to Australia, but I don't want you to worry about me because I know what I'm doing."

She hung up before adding, "I think."

Harry arrived an hour later, looking like a *Gentlemen's Quarterly* model in his elegantly cut navy-blue suit. When he saw her luggage sitting in the entryway, he arched one dark eyebrow and favored her with one of his nuclear grins.

"Let's go, love," he said, reaching down to take the handle of one suitcase in each hand. Rumpel purred and curled around Harry's left ankle. "You have, I presume, made arrangements for the cat?"

"Mrs. Ingallstadt will look after Rumpel," Amy said, and even as she spoke she could hardly believe she was really doing this crazy, impulsive thing. She had always been the practical type, the one who balanced her checkbook to the penny and color-coded her sock drawer.

Harry's blue gaze drifted over her simple cotton print dress with unsettling leisure. "Mmm. Well, then, we're off."

They drove to the airport in Harry's rented van, and Amy gnawed at her lower lip through practically the whole trip. Once in a while, she even reached for the door handle in an impotent stab at making a run for it.

Harry seemed amused.

"I suppose you're used to women who do this sort of thing all the time," Amy said in stiff and testy tones, clutching at her anger as though it were a lifeline.

He chuckled. "What sort of thing is that, my lovely?" he teased, pulling the van to a stop next to a sleek jet that stood gleaming on the tarmac beside a private hangar.

"This is not at all like me," Amy insisted, when Harry came around to her side to help her down.

He made an answering sound, a low rumble in his throat, and then brushed her lips ever so lightly with his own. "Which is one of the many things that makes you so blasted appealing," he agreed with a philosophical sigh. For the first time, Amy realized that Harry didn't want this attraction between them any more than she did.

The idea was oddly painful, all things considered.

The pilot had already arrived and was in the process of a preflight check when Harry gave Amy a tour of the aircraft. There was a galley, glittering and efficient, and all the leather-upholstered seats were cushy and wide, built to swivel on their shiny steel bases. There was a bar, which didn't interest Amy—just the thought of combining liquor with altitude made her queasy.

"There are water closets back there," Harry said, gesturing toward a wide hallway at the rear of the cabin. "Take your choice."

For Amy, in those moments, curiosity was a refuge, a place she could scurry into and hide out from her fear of the inevitable. She ventured into the hallway and peered through two separate doorways.

Even though Amy's father was a heart surgeon, and she'd never known poverty in her life, those glitzy bathrooms came as a surprise to her, with their glass and marble.

Harry went past her with the suitcases, disappearing into yet another room. The master suite, no doubt.

The magnetism was powerful, and resisting it took a formidable effort, but Amy managed to grope her way back to the main cabin. She was standing behind one of the elegant seats, her fingers digging deep into the sumptuous upholstery, when Harry returned.

She smiled shakily. "You certainly have nice bathrooms," she said. The instant the words had left her mouth she longed to call them back, they sounded so silly.

Harry chuckled. "Yes," he agreed. His indigo eyes moved over her in a way that was, incomprehensibly, both arrogant and reverent.

Amy felt as though he'd deftly peeled her clothes away, and it seemed to her that the very air was pulsating with some elemental, unseen force—a power that emanated from Harry himself.

The intercom saved her from having to speak, which was fortunate because a troupe of heated fantasies had invaded her mind, crowding out all rational thought.

"The preflight check has been completed, sir," announced the pilot's voice, "and we have clearance for takeoff."

Harry walked over to the bar and pushed a button on a high-tech unit behind it, and his soul-searing gaze never left Amy once. "Fine," he said in a voice that was somewhat hoarse. "Thank you."

He crossed the cabin then and, smiling slightly, pressed Amy into a seat. The act of crouching beside her and fastening her seat belt was entirely innocent, and yet it left Amy feeling as though they'd engaged in half an hour of intense foreplay.

Harry took the seat nearest hers and fastened himself in. It was plain enough to Amy that he hadn't missed the significance of her bright eyes and flushed face.

Soon the plane was speeding down the runway. Harry held Amy's hand until they were aloft.

"There now," he said, unsnapping his seat belt and rising as casually as he might from an easy chair in his living room. "We're on our way. Would you like something to drink?"

Yes, Amy thought. *A double shot of the strongest whiskey you have.* "A diet cola would be nice," she said aloud.

Harry made no comment on her choice; he simply went about taking a can of soda from the refrigerator beneath the bar.

Amy unfastened her seat belt and thrust herself shakily to her feet. There was no going back now.

She crossed to the teakwood bar, which was bolted securely to the floor, and leaned against it, trying to look as though she did this sort of thing all the time.

"You must practically live in this plane, it's outfitted so well," she commented.

Harry was still behind the bar, and he handed Amy her cola. Then he grinned his endearing, soul-wrenching grin and said with a shrug, "I'm rich."

A nervous giggle escaped Amy, and she just barely kept herself from slapping one hand over her mouth. She'd never been more sober in her life, and yet she felt as though she were roaring drunk.

"Relax, Amy," Harry said, leaning forward slightly, bracing himself against the bar with wide-spread hands. "I'm not planning to heave you over one shoulder, haul you off to my bed and ravish you. When we make love—and we will, God help us—it will be because the desire is mutual.''

Although Amy was relieved by this declaration, she was also damnably disappointed. And she certainly would have been better off without the caveman images Harry had just planted in her mind.

"Did you do that on purpose?" she demanded, only realizing she'd spoken the thought aloud when Harry laughed and answered her.

"Do what, love?" he countered, rounding the bar and laying his hands on either side of her narrow waist.

Amy swallowed hard. She was a nineties woman, liberated and successful in her own right, but she couldn't help imagining what it would be like to be hoisted over Harry's shoulder like the willing captive of some sexy pirate. "Oh, God," she groaned.

Harry bent his head and tasted her mouth as though it were some rare and priceless delicacy, to be enjoyed at leisure.

Amy's heart began to pound and her breathing was audible.

Harry's lips strayed to her throat, the tender hollow beneath her ear. He took the glass from her hand and set it on the bar.

Amy's traitorous body was already preparing itself to receive him, already pleading for a fulfillment that had been denied it for over two years. "Oh, God," she said again, when Harry's hands cupped her breasts.

His thumbs made her nipples go taut against the soft cotton of her sundress.

"Maybe," he speculated huskily, from the tingling space between Amy's shoulder and the base of her neck, "we'd better do something about this."

"D-do something about what?" Amy's voice trembled, like her body. The rumblings of an impending spiritual and emotional quake were making cracks in the wall she'd built around her innermost self, while, on the surface of her skin, a million tiny nerves quivered.

Harry touched the tip of his tongue to the corner of her mouth, and Amy had a melting sensation. In another minute, she'd be all over his shoes, like warm wax.

"About this attraction between us," he finally replied. Between light, teasing kisses, he added, "Amy, we're not going to have a moment's peace until we've made love."

The last of Amy's defenses crumbled then; she knew Harry was right. "Yes," was all she could manage to say, she was so overcome, so confused, so in need.

He lifted her easily, gently, into his arms and started toward the hallway and the one room Amy hadn't dared to explore earlier.

"Will the pilot know?" she asked warily.

Harry kissed the top of her head and chuckled. "No, love. Not unless you turn on the intercom."

The master bedroom was surprisingly spacious, even considering the luxurious proportions of that airplane. The floor was carpeted, the lighting dim, the air subtly tinged with Harry's very distinctive scent.

He set Amy on her feet at the foot of the bed and pushed a tendril of hair back from her cheek with a gentle forefinger.

"You're sure?" he asked.

She nodded, unable to speak, though every word in every dictionary in the world seemed to be waiting at the back of her mind, wanting to be part of some enormous declaration she couldn't begin to make.

He unzipped her sundress and eased the fabric down over her shoulders. When the dress was gone, Harry caught one finger under her bra strap and brought that down, too. She sucked in her breath and tilted her head back in surrender when he bent to sample her nipple as he'd tasted her lips earlier.

Tears trickled over Amy's temples and into her hair, not because she was ashamed or unhappy, but because it felt so wondrously good to give herself in this age-old way.

Presently, Harry bared her other breast and gave it proper and thorough attention, having tossed her bra aside. She was wearing only her satiny tap pants when he laid her on the bed.

The velvet softness of hundreds of rose petals cushioned her fevered flesh, and their lush scent perfumed the room. Amy was transfixed as she watched Harry strip away his clothes.

His body was lean and magnificent as he stretched out beside her. Taking a handful of the scattered pink, yellow and white petals, he sprinkled them over her and then bent to kiss the places where they landed. As he did this, he took her tap pants down over her hips and thighs, and they were lost in the blanket of blossoms.

Harry covered Amy with petals, and with the touch of each one to her quivering skin, she wanted him more.

"Harry, please," she finally rasped in desperation.

He raised her knees and knelt between them. He burrowed and nuzzled his way through the blossoms that sheltered her most vulnerable place, then scored her boldly with his tongue.

Amy gave a primitive groan of welcoming surrender and arched her back. Harry held her taut bottom in his hands and drank from her greedily.

Delirious with a terrifying, sweeping pleasure, Amy tossed her head from side to side. One forearm rested across her mouth, muffling the soft cries of wonderment and glory that she couldn't hold back.

And still Harry consumed her.

Finally, with a shout of joyous desolation, Amy reached her climax.

Even as he lowered her back to the flower-strewn mattress, Harry kissed the insides of Amy's thighs and the smooth moistness of her belly. She was beyond speech, beyond thought; all she could do was lie there in Harry's arms, her head resting on his strong chest. As pieces of her soul gradually wandered back from the far reaches of the universe, where her shattering release had flung them, Harry lightly caressed her shoulder blades, the small of her back, her bottom, her thighs.

Presently, he laid her on her back and settled his powerful frame between her legs. It seemed to Amy that every muscle in her body had melted—she could not possibly respond to this final stage of Harry's lovemaking—but she longed to be joined with him. The desire was far more complex than mere physical need.

He paused at the portal of her womanhood and looked deeply into her eyes, silently asking her permission.

Amy nodded, tilted her head back, and closed her eyes.

Harry moved into her in a powerful stroke that awakened all her satisfied senses to an even keener need than before.

Amy's eyes flew open again, in startled surprise, and her fingers rushed to Harry's hard, sun-browned shoulders.

"Do you want me to stop?" he asked quietly, his manhood buried deep within her.

"No," Amy whispered in a frantic rush, shaking her head.

He withdrew slowly, until their joining was almost broken, and Amy felt genuine despair. But then Harry took her forcefully and she was completely, joyously lost.

As her body convulsed beneath his in the final moments of Harry's conquest, her cries echoed off the back of his throat.

Moments after she'd settled back to the mattress, completely exhausted, Harry wedged his hands under her hips to press her closer still. With a low groan, he faced his own moment of utter surrender.

At least half an hour must have passed before either of them had the breath to speak.

"Rose petals, huh?" Amy said, staring up at the ceiling. "You were pretty sure of yourself, weren't you?"

Harry was propped up beside her on one elbow. With the fingers of his other hand, he caressed a responsive nipple. "I was pretty sure of *you*," he countered.

Amy was holding a lot of things at bay in those moments. Like reality, for instance. "The flowers were a poetic touch," she said. "I guess you probably do that every time you bring a woman here."

He was silent for a long interval, during which he continued to tease her nipples, each in turn, with skillful fingers. "I've brought women to this bed before, of course," he said finally, unapologetically. "But those rose petals were for you and you alone, Amy."

What a line, observed the left side of Amy's brain. *If this is a dream, don't let me wake up,* countered the whimsical right side.

As if to prove his assertion, Harry gathered a handful of the bruised, fragrant petals and began to rub them lightly against Amy's breasts and belly.

She moaned helplessly as he lowered his mouth to her nipple, once again to drink from her.

* * *

They landed in San Francisco some two hours later and although Amy's knees were still wobbly from Harry's lovemaking, she'd managed to grab a shower in one of the fancy airplane bathrooms and put on evening clothes.

She wore a snowy-soft white jacket, with tiny iridescent beads stitched to it to lend a subtle sparkle, a delicate camisole top, and black silk slacks.

As she and Harry descended the roll-away stairs to the tarmac, a pearl-gray limousine whisked to a stop beside the plane.

"Wow," Amy said. "You really know how to impress a girl."

Harry's grin was downright wicked. "You did seem pretty impressed," he agreed, and Amy knew he was referring to her unbridled responses to his lovemaking.

She felt a little anticipatory thrill, because she knew she would return to Harry's bed that night.

They dined in a restaurant atop one of San Francisco's finest hotels, and since the requisite fog had somehow failed to roll in, the view of the harbor and the Golden Gate Bridge was unobstructed.

Amy had seafood of some kind—she would never remember exactly what—and she indulged in one glass of white wine. The sweet, pulsing daze she'd been wandering in turned to a feeling of giddy adventurousness.

She wanted to neck in the rear of the limousine while they were driving back to the airport, but she was too shy to make the first move, and all Harry did was hold her hand and look at her as though she were a poem he wanted to memorize. Or a puzzle he couldn't solve.

They had barely returned to the jet when two men in suits appeared. Harry obviously knew them, but they produced Customs badges anyway, and Amy showed them her passport. She was heart-stoppingly certain they were going to say she couldn't leave the country.

"Have a good flight," one of them said to Amy with a smile, while the other shook hands with Harry.

When the Customs agents were gone, Harry went to the cockpit to confer with the pilot. Amy strapped herself in and waited.

After a few minutes, Harry's voice came over the intercom. "Sit tight, love," he said. "The flight check has been completed and we're about to take off."

They'd been airborne almost half an hour when Harry finally returned to the main cabin. With a chuckle he unfastened Amy's seat belt and pried her fingers loose from the arm rests.

"You're as beautiful as a moonflower," he said, holding her close and burrowing into the soft skin of her neck. "And despite the shower and that perfume you're wearing, I can still catch the scent of the rose petals."

He left her, just briefly, to dim the cabin lights and turn on soft music. Then Harry drew Amy into his arms and they danced, and for Amy that was almost as keenly erotic as lying naked in a bed of flower petals.

Emotionally, Amy was drowning. She thought of Tyler, in a desperate attempt to anchor herself to the only world she really knew, but suddenly he was only a sweet, fading memory.

The music went on and on, and Harry and Amy danced tirelessly. Then he took her hand and led her back to his bed.

Where before their lovemaking had had a fevered urgency, now it was leisurely and deliberate. Harry brought Amy to one release after another before he permitted her the final conquering she literally begged for, and the first light of dawn was sparkling on the blue waters of the sea when he finally allowed her to sleep.

The thump and lurch of landing brought her bolt upright in bed, her eyes wide. Harry was fully dressed, wearing charcoal slacks and a lightweight white sweater, his sleek, raven-black hair glistening in the morning light.

"Where are we?" Amy asked, pulling the sheets up under her chin even though she knew it was too late to hide herself from Harry.

"Honolulu," he answered, grinning at her rumpled hair and dazed expression. "We'll only be here long enough to refuel, do some maintenance and change pilots, so take your time getting dressed."

Blushing to recall how she'd behaved with this man, how she'd let him shape and maneuver her into every possible position for taking, Amy tried to get out of bed without letting go of the sheet. She wanted the blue terry cloth robe draped over a nearby chair, but Harry got to it before she did and held it out of reach.

"On second thought," he said, his dark blue eyes full of mischief and passion, "don't bother to get dressed at all."

bed without letting go of the sheet. She walked the
blue terry cloth robe draped over a nearby chair ...
Harry got to [...] the bed and held it out ...
"Oh, a robe, actually," he said, his dark blue eyes
full of laughter and passion ... they looked, to say
the least of all.

Six

Amy settled into the airplane's big marble bathtub
with a contented sigh. The intercom crackled out the
announcement that the flight had been cleared for
takeoff, and she gripped the sides of the tub as the
craft hurtled down the runway and then catapulted
into the air.

Some of Amy's bubbly bathwater slopped over onto
the floor.

"They should have put a seatbelt in this thing," she
muttered.

Harry's laughter came over the intercom, along with
a few chuckles from the pilot.

"Push the white button on the panel, love," Harry
told her. "*After* you get out of the tub."

Red in the face, Amy snatched up a towel and scrambled out. She could hardly get to the intercom panel fast enough.

Once Amy was dried off and dressed, her hair toweled and then combed into a casual style, she made the bed. The crushed rose petals had mysteriously disappeared, but their luscious scent lingered.

Amy ventured out into the main cabin. She sat contentedly at one of the windows for a long time, looking down on the clouds—giant cotton balls stretched thin—as well as the sea, just enjoying the view.

She was surprised when Harry showed up, carrying a tray. He'd brought her a gigantic fruit salad, a croissant and a little pot of special Hawaiian coffee.

Amy gratefully accepted the food, but her tone of voice was testy. "Do the rest of the intercoms on this plane have minds of their own, or just the one in that particular bathroom?"

Harry grinned and sat down in another seat, facing her. He was wearing jeans and a light yellow sports shirt, but he still looked elegant enough to play for high stakes in Monaco. "No worries, love. That's the only one with temperament."

Amy popped a juicy piece of fresh pineapple into her mouth and looked out at the sea.

"What are you thinking?" Harry asked softly at great length.

She sighed, gazing at him with bewildered eyes. "I guess I'm waiting for the guilt to strike."

He took a strawberry from her bowl and touched it lightly to her lips. Amy opened her mouth to receive the tidbit and felt a sweet tension begin to curl up tight within her.

"Why would you feel guilty?" he asked quietly.

Amy was practically breathless. She was going to have to talk to Debbie when she got back to Seattle, find out why a simple thing like having a man put a strawberry to her lips felt so much like a sweet seduction.

"Because of Tyler," she said lamely. "Oh, I know we haven't done anything wrong." She wanted to tell Harry about her strange encounters with Ty, but she was afraid of the impression that would make.

Harry raised both eyebrows. "Well, then?"

"It's just that, well, I'd never been with anyone else—until you."

Resting his elbows on the arms of his chair, Harry made a finger steeple beneath his chin. He sat quietly, ready to listen, and if Amy hadn't already been crazy about him, that gesture would have done it.

"Instead of guilt," Amy stumbled on awkwardly, "I feel a sense of adventure and newness and excitement. Like, maybe I'm something more than a mother and an erstwhile wife."

Harry's dark brows knitted together in a momentary frown. "Maybe?"

Amy bit into a grape, chewing thoughtfully and then swallowing. "Tyler was a great guy," she finally said with a shaky sigh. "And God knows, I loved him. But I don't think it ever occurred to either of us that I should have an identity apart from being a wife and mother."

"Mmm," Harry said.

Amy laughed. "If you ever get tired of being a venture capitalist, or whatever you are, you could be a shrink. You listen very well."

He took another strawberry between his fingers and traced the outline of her mouth with the morsel until her lips parted. Just when Amy thought surely he was going to take her to his bed, he asked, "How would you like to try your hand at flying the plane?"

Although her first instinct was to draw back and shake her head no, Amy made herself nod.

Moments later, she was in the cockpit, in the copilot's seat, wearing earphones and staring at the instrument panel in utter ignorance. The pilot had gone to the rear of the aircraft, and Harry was occupying his chair.

Over the next hour he taught Amy the function of most of the instruments and showed her how to gain and lose altitude. For a while, she was actually flying the aircraft herself, and the knowledge filled her with a kind of pride she'd never felt before.

Finally, however, Amy excused herself and left the copilot's seat to the man who had come on board in Honolulu. She found a book in Harry's room and settled into one of the comfortable seats in the main cabin to read.

Lunchtime came, and Harry clattered around in the galley, opening and shutting doors. A bell chimed, and he carried a tray forward to the pilot, then brought

Amy a compact meal of Spanish rice and vegetables, along with a plate for himself.

They ate in comfortable silence, not needing to talk, and then Harry went back to the cockpit. Amy tidied up the galley, thinking that was the least she could do, since Harry had done the cooking, then returned to her book.

She was so absorbed in the story, a fast-paced spy thriller, that when Harry appeared, she was startled.

He took the book from her hands and set it aside, then unsnapped her seat belt. Again, Amy was electrified by a perfectly ordinary thing.

She knew what Harry wanted, and she wanted it, too, but the vamp in her made her offer a token resistance.

"What if I don't go to bed with you?" she whispered. Even though the blood was thundering in her ears, Amy hadn't forgotten the incident with the bathroom intercom, and she wasn't taking any chances on having the pilot overhear such an intimate conversation.

Harry ran his hands lightly over her thighs, easing her legs apart at the same time. "Then I'll have you right here," he said, his voice low, like thunder rumbling in a summer sky. After that, he kissed her, subjecting her to a preliminary conquering with his tongue. Then he bared her breasts.

"I'll go," Amy moaned, as he nibbled at her. "I'll go!"

Harry chuckled and lifted her legs, so that her knees rested over the arms of the seat. Then he opened the snap on her jeans.

"Harry," she pleaded.

He bent to nip at the crux of her womanhood and, despite the sturdy denim covering her, Amy felt the contact to the core of her being. She closed her eyes, loving the feeling of his hands cupping her breasts, and let her hips rise and fall as he bid them.

After tormenting her for at least fifteen minutes, he took her legs from the arms of the chair and relieved her of her jeans and panties, then put her back into position again. The first foray of his tongue tore a raw cry from her throat, but Harry granted no quarter. He slipped his hands under her bottom and then feasted in earnest.

When the first wave of satisfaction struck, Amy was grateful, because the sensations Harry was treating her to were so intense they were almost frightening. But that crest was followed by a second, higher one, and then a third.

As Amy shuddered with the volcanic force of her pleasure, she clasped Harry's shoulders in both hands. Her vision blurred and she cried out at the top of her lungs, but there was no helping that. She was totally out of control.

Her heart had almost settled back into its normal rate when he gathered her up and carried her to his bed.

The taking of Amy Ryan had only begun.

* * *

They landed in Fiji, then briefly, hours later, in Auckland, New Zealand, then in Sydney, where more Customs men came on board and inspected Amy's passport. Finally, they headed north again.

When Amy finally stepped off the plane, into a lush tropical climate, she was amazed to see colorful parrots flying free, as robins did at home in Seattle. The sea was as blue as India ink, lapping at sugar-white beaches, and a spectacular stone house loomed in the distance, as imposing as a castle.

"Where are we?" Amy asked, still in a fog from all the sweet, busy hours spent in Harry's bed.

He laughed and kissed her softly on the mouth. "Paradise," he answered. "The island is named Eden, and not without reason."

A Jeep was waiting at the edge of the private airstrip, and Harry flung the suitcases into the back with a practiced motion, then helped Amy onto the seat. The pilot was evidently staying behind to perform maintenance on the plane.

There was a working fountain in front of the house, and two Australian sheepdogs came bouncing across the yard, barking gleefully, to greet their master.

Harry took a moment to acknowledge the animals, then lifted Amy down from the Jeep.

"You'll be needing a bath and something to eat," he said, his accent sounding more pronounced than before. "Then you'll want to catch up on all that sleep I've deprived you of since we left Seattle."

An amiable housekeeper opened one of the stately double doors, and Amy stepped inside. She didn't notice much about Harry's house that first day, because she was too tired and distracted, and she was grateful when he led her upstairs to an airy suite filled with the distant sound of the tide.

He undressed her, like a child, and they showered together. Even as Harry tenderly soaped and rinsed her exhausted body, Amy could barely keep her eyes open.

At last, he wrapped her in a soft, giant towel and took her to bed. After pulling a T-shirt over her head, he tucked her under the covers and bent to kiss her forehead.

"Sleep well, love," he said.

Dimly, Amy was aware of Harry moving around the room, getting dressed again, and she wanted him beside her even though she hadn't the strength for even one more session of lovemaking.

"Harry," she whimpered, patting the mattress fitfully with one hand.

He chuckled. "No, love, not today. You're too tired."

Amy fought to open her eyes, marshalled all her strength to ask, "What about you? Aren't...you tired?"

Harry bent and planted a smacking kiss on her forehead. "On the contrary, my sweet little Yankee, I feel like I could take on the world with one hand lashed behind my back."

"Don't...go."

"Sleep," he ordered with mock sternness. Then he was gone and Amy slept.

The room was bright with sunshine when she awakened, alone in the big bed and fully rested. Her suitcase was nowhere in sight, but when Amy opened the top drawer of a beautiful antique bureau, she found some of her clothes neatly stacked inside.

Quickly she dressed. Beyond the glass doors leading onto the terrace, parrots made their raucous cawing sound and the tide recited its ancient, rhythmic poetry. After brushing her teeth, grooming her hair and applying lip gloss, Amy ventured out of the bedroom.

She was ravenously hungry and nervous because there was no sign of Harry in any of the enormous, rustic rooms that lay between his room and the kitchen.

The familiar housekeeper was there, stirring batter in a crockery bowl, and she greeted Amy with a gapped smile.

"There you are, then," the woman chirped gleefully. "If I hadn't seen you arriving with me own eyes just yesterday, I would have sworn you were nothing but a story our Harry had made up."

Amy was embarrassed, but she made an effort to be cordial. "My name is Amy Ryan," she said.

"Elsa O'Donnell," said the housekeeper, with a nod and a twinkly smile. "You'd be Master Tyler's widow, then. Oh my, but we was fond of that boy."

The reminder of her husband unsettled Amy a little. As much as she'd loved Tyler, she'd never responded to him in quite the way she did with Harry. She just nodded.

"Sit down," Elsa commanded good-naturedly, setting the mixing bowl aside. "I'll see about getting you some tea."

Amy glanced at the clock and saw that it was two-fifteen. She'd not only slept away the night, but a good part of the day as well.

By tea, Elsa meant a scone with jam and fresh cream, a plate of fruit, four delicate sandwiches and a pot of rich orange pekoe.

Amy consumed the repast as politely as she could, considering that she was famished, then asked shyly, "Is Harry around?"

"He's down at the beach, I imagine," answered Elsa, methodically putting away the ingredients of afternoon tea. "Headed straight for it after getting you settled yesterday, and was off to the water again this morning, right after breakfast."

Amy rinsed her cup and plate and silverware at the sink, then set them on the drain board. "If I walk down there, will I find him?"

"It's a big island," Elsa replied. "But I think you'll run across him. Just mind you don't go through the cane fields—there's snakes there."

Amy shuddered, but even the thought of snakes didn't dampen her excitement at being in a new place and, yes, the prospect of seeing Harry again had its attractions, too.

The sheepdogs joined her on the lawn, romping along beside her, and they were the ones who led her to Harry. He was in water up to his hips, examining the hull of a sleek sailboat, and his grin was as dazzling as the tropical sun.

"So then, Sleeping Beauty has awakened," he teased, making his way toward her. He wasn't wearing a shirt, just cutoffs dark and sodden and clingy with seawater. "Welcome to the land of Oz."

Amy, wearing shorts and a T-shirt herself, kicked off her sandals so she could feel the fine, pristine sand between her toes.

Harry met her on the beach, and his kiss, quick and innocent as it was, sent her senses tumbling in all directions, just as always. He curled two fingers under her chin and grinned again.

"If you're all rested up, love, I'd like to volunteer to wear you out again."

Amy laughed and twisted away from him, running toward the sparkling turquoise water. The dogs bounded after her, barking with delight at the game.

She and Harry splashed each other in the lapping tide, and Amy felt as though all the grief had been erased from her past, leaving only the joy.

"Who else lives on this island?" she asked later, when the two of them were sitting on the beach, their feet buried in the sand.

Harry brushed a tendril of hair back from her forehead. "Just Elsa and her husband, Shelt. He's the gardener."

Amy lay back with a sigh, looking up at an impossibly blue sky. Exotic flowers bloomed at the edges of the cove, orange ones, pink, violet and white. Birds that would only be seen in pet stores and zoos at home chattered in the trees, crazy splotches of living color.

"This really is a garden of Eden," she said, recalling what Harry had said when they'd first arrived on the island. "I wish we could stay here forever."

Harry stretched out beside her and gave her a brief but tantalizing kiss. "There's no reason why we can't. Live here with me, Amy. We'll start the world all over again."

Amy blinked, and her throat tightened with emotion. "I can't do that," she said. "I have two children, remember? They need to go to school and spend time with their friends and with Tyler's family."

Harry shrugged. "We'd live in the States half the year anyway, love. We could hire a nanny to look after Oliver and Ashley here on the island, and the Ryans would be welcome to visit at any time. They know that." He paused, gazing pensively out to sea. "There are worse things than growing up in paradise, you know."

Deep down, Amy knew Oliver and Ashley would be happy here. They adored Harry, just as she did, and his island would seem like heaven on earth to them. When he got bored with domestic life, however, and wanted to return to the jet set, they'd be shattered.

Losing Tyler had been enough trauma. Playing Swiss Family Robinson for a few months or years, then being abandoned again, would crush Oliver and Ashley, maybe destroy their ability to trust.

"I want a ride in the sailboat," Amy announced, as much to change the subject as anything.

"Tomorrow," Harry promised. He seemed troubled, distracted.

That night, it rained as it can only rain in the tropics. The droplets were warm as bathwater, and Amy stood on the terrace outside Harry's room, her face turned upward and her arms outspread to welcome the deluge.

"You're daft," Harry accused, but he laughed and kissed Amy and soon he was drenched, just as she was.

When he finally hauled her inside the house and began toweling her dry, she saw that the bed was literally mounded with orchidlike blossoms. Some were pink, some white, but all were beautiful.

A sweet ache constricted Amy's throat, and she stood still while Harry peeled away her sodden clothes, then his own. Finally, he laid her on the bed of flowers and made slow, gentle love to her.

In the morning it was as though the rain had never fallen, so fiercely did the sun shine on the sea and the dazzling sand. Amy awakened slowly, cushioned in crushed petals, but this time when she reached out, Harry was beside her.

"When are we going home?" she asked, dreading the answer. If it hadn't been for Oliver and Ashley, she would gladly have agreed to live on the island for the rest of her life.

Harry rolled onto his side and kissed her breast. "Never," he replied throatily. "Consider yourself kidnapped, a one-woman harem."

"Just promise never to give me back," she whispered, "no matter how high the ransom gets."

Moments later, ransom was the farthest thing from Amy's mind. She was into unconditional surrender.

After a leisurely shower together, and an equally unhurried breakfast in the kitchen, Harry and Amy took the picnic basket Elsa had packed and set out for the nearby cove where the sailboat was moored.

"Take your clothes off," Harry ordered, when they reached the shore.

"Already?" Amy countered, eyeing him skeptically.

He laughed. "Yes. If you don't want to get them wet when you wade out to the boat." With that, Harry removed his cut-offs and T-shirt, rolled the garments up and secured them under the handles of the wicker picnic basket. Balancing that on top of his head, he stepped into the water, magnificently naked.

Amy was considerably more self-conscious about stripping, even though she knew they were completely alone on that magical beach. Nonetheless, she followed Harry's lead, took off everything and marched into the water.

After tossing the basket onto the deck, Harry vaulted over the side and reached down to help Amy in after him. The weathered old boards were smooth and warm from the sun.

Amy could have languished there for a while, but Harry gave her a playful swat on the bottom and said, "What's this? A mutiny before we even weigh anchor?"

Hastily, Amy rose and put her clothes back on, except for her shoes.

After a few minutes of busy preparation, they set sail.

"Where are we going?" Amy inquired, shading her eyes with one hand.

"That island over there," Harry answered, pointing.

Amy felt like an intrepid explorer. All her life she'd taken the safe and practical route, whenever a choice was offered. Now here she was in a foreign country, with a man she'd known only briefly, about to set sail in tropical seas.

So what if their destination was clearly in sight?

The water between Eden Island and its neighbor was so clear that Amy could see the reefs beneath the surface and the colorful fish that swam through intricate passages. When she saw a shark glide by, she drew back from the side of the boat, her mind filled with movie images.

Harry, who was working with the sails, smiled at her reaction. "What did you see, love? A great white?"

Amy felt the blood drain from her cheeks. "Do you mean to tell me that *Jaws* might be swimming around down there, at this very moment?"

Harry laughed. "A famous shark like that? Not likely, rose petal. He's living in the South of France and wearing sunglasses so his fans won't recognize him."

"Very funny," Amy replied grudgingly, peeking over the side of the boat again. The spectacle going on down there was just too good to miss.

When they reached the other island—if it had a name of its own, Harry didn't mention it—Amy was possessed by a remarkably pleasant feeling that she and Harry were completely alone on the planet.

The only sign that anyone else had ever visited the island before was a tree house wedged between two massive palms. Small boards had been nailed to the trunk of one of the trees to form a crude ladder, and the structure's thick roof appeared to have been woven from long, supple leaves.

"Yours?" Amy inquired.

Harry looked away. "I built it for my stepdaughter, Eireen. Unfortunately, Madeline—my wife—never gave the poor little thing a chance to be a child."

Amy touched his arm lightly, then pushed up nonexistent sleeves—she was wearing a T-shirt—and started up the ladder.

"Best let me go first, love," Harry remarked presently, when she'd climbed about five rungs. "Could be snakes up there."

Amy was back on the ground with the speed and dispatch of a cartoon character. "Snakes?" she croaked.

Harry took a manly stance for effect, then began to climb deftly toward the tree house, the picnic basket in one hand. There was a rustling sound, followed by a fallout of leaves and dirt, then Harry peered down at her from a crudely shaped, glassless window.

"All clear, rose petal," he called.

Amy ran her tongue over her dry lips and then stepped onto the first rung, gripping another with both hands.

Although there were no snakes in the tree house, it was clear enough that other things had been nesting in there. For all of that, it was a lot of fun, yet another thing Amy had never done before.

"Come here," Harry said, and Amy went straight into his arms. It did not even occur to her to resist.

His kiss was one of thorough mastery; the slow dance of their tongues soon became a duel of passion. Amy felt as though a sudden fever had set in, and by the time Harry had removed her T-shirt, then her bra, then the rest of her clothes, she was weak with the need to surrender.

He enjoyed her, like some juicy tropical fruit, for a long, torturously sweet interval, wringing response after response from her. When he finally made her his own, she came apart in his arms as uninhibited as a jungle tigress with her mate.

After her senses were restored, Amy found herself lying on the floor of the tree house, where Harry had spread a soft blanket taken from the picnic basket. While Harry caressed her—he was lying quietly beside her, still recovering from his own invasion of heaven—Amy felt strong enough to permit herself memories of lovemaking with Tyler.

Her late husband had been a tender, considerate lover always, and Amy had learned a woman's secrets in his arms. She had to admit, though, that there had never been the sense of wild abandon she felt with Harry. It was a different sort of passion, more mature and more intense.

And far more dangerous.

He slid down to kiss the flat of her stomach. "Stay with me, Amy," he said hoarsely. "Please."

Harry had never said "I love you," nor had he asked her to be his wife. Amy was pretty sure he was marriage-shy after his first experience, and a sophisticated man of the world like him would *expect* an uncomplicated relationship with no strings attached.

"I can't," she said, as a soft tropical rain began to patter on the roof of dried leaves. She'd loved being married; Tyler had shown her just how marvelous a physical and spiritual partnership could be. For the first time since his death, Amy felt ready to make a real and lasting commitment to someone new.

They ate their picnic lunch naked, cozy inside the dank and dusty tree house, talking quietly, but the day had lost some of its magic.

When the rain let up, late that afternoon, they returned to the boat and sailed back to Harry's island.

Harry made a fire on the living-room hearth, because the rain had returned and there was a slight chill in the air.

That night, for the first time since their adventure had begun, Harry and Amy didn't make love.

They spent the next two days walking the beaches, soaking up the medicinal Queensland sun, playing backgammon on the terrace. Lying next to each other at night, they were unable to resist the magnetism, and while their lovemaking was as ferociously satisfying as ever, there was a distance about it. A certain reserve.

Amy's heart was heavy when they left the island on the morning of the third day; she thought she knew now how Eve must have felt when she and Adam had been driven from the Garden.

Harry kept himself busy in the cockpit of the jet, while Amy wandered aimlessly around the cabin, wishing the dream never had to end.

They landed in Sydney a few hours later, and Harry returned from the controls.

"You'll need an evening gown if you brought one," he said, as though speaking to a casual acquaintance instead of a woman he'd made love to in beds of flowers and in a tree house.

They rode downtown in yet another limousine, over the famous bridge, and their hotel suite boasted a view of the Opera House and the harbor.

Still, the mood was subdued, and Amy couldn't help thinking that, glamorous surroundings or none, Cinderella time was over. The glass slipper wasn't going to fit.

Seven

Harry Griffith was a man who planned his life years in advance. He knew details about his future other people wouldn't even begin to consider until they'd passed the age of sixty.

One thing he had definitely *not* planned on, however, was falling in love.

He turned from the window overlooking Sydney Harbor when he sensed Amy's presence, and the sight of her standing there in her light blue, sleek-fitting dress practically stopped his heart. Still, cool reserve was Harry's strong point; he'd relied on the trait for so long that it was second nature to him now.

Amy's eyes were bright with a peculiar mixture of defiance and hope, and Harry made up his mind in that moment that he would sacrifice anything to have her for his own. His pride, his fortune—anything.

He took her to see *Madame Butterfly* at the Opera House, and then the two of them had dinner in an out-of-the-way restaurant Harry had always favored.

"What did you think of the opera?" Harry finally asked. The question came out smoothly, as the things he said nearly always did, but behind the facade his emotions were churning in secret.

Amy took a sip of her wine before answering. "I've seen it before, of course," she replied, looking uncomfortable. "I always cry and I always get angry because Pinkerton shows so little regard for Butterfly's feelings. He goes into the marriage planning to dump her later, for a 'real wife.'"

Harry felt a rhythmic, thumping headache begin behind his right temple. Only when it was too late, when they'd already taken their seats in the Opera House, had he realized that *Madame Butterfly* was probably a poor choice because it dealt with the subject of male treachery.

"All men aren't like Pinkerton, of course," he said quietly.

Amy didn't look convinced. "When a man travels a lot," she said distractedly, "there are temptations. I have a friend who used to be married to an airline pilot, and he had a playmate in every city between here and Buffalo, New York."

Harry arched an eyebrow. "Busy man," he allowed. "Amy, what is it? What's really troubling you?"

He saw the battle going on behind her beautiful hazel eyes and wondered whether he was winning or losing.

"I think I'm in love with you," she said, as though confessing that she'd contracted some embarrassing disease.

Staid, sedate Harry Griffith. It was all he could do not to leap onto his chair and shout the news to everyone in the restaurant. "That's a problem?" he asked.

"Yes!" she whispered furiously. "You're a rich man! You have your own jet and a private island!"

"I'll try to reform," Harry promised.

Amy's cheeks glowed pink, and her wondrous eyes were now glistening with tears. "I can't share you with all the other women you probably know. I won't!"

"You don't have to," he said reasonably.

She stared at him for a moment. "What?"

"Amy, you're not the only one who's fallen in love here."

She dropped her fork. "You're saying that you— that I—that we—"

"I love you, Amy. I thought you understood that when I kept asking you to stay with me—I believe I said something poetic about our starting a new world together."

She picked up her fork again and waved it like a baton. Her mouth moved, as though she would deliver a lecture, but no sound came out.

"I'm asking you to marry me," Harry said, figuring he'd better grab the opportunity to speak while her tongue was still tangled. "I'll sell the island and we'll spend all our time in the States. I'll wear baseball caps, drink beer and call you 'babe,' if that's what you want. And even though it goes without saying, I'm going to say it anyway—I'll never be unfaithful to you."

A tear scurried down Amy's cheek. "You'll get tired of us, Ashley and Oliver and me."

"No way," Harry answered, his voice sounding hoarse. "Amy, men *are* capable of making solid commitments. You know that. Tyler did."

She obviously had no argument. Tyler had made her happy, and Harry blessed his late friend for that, silently promising Ty, as well as himself, that he would never bring Amy anything but joy.

"I wouldn't want you to sell the island," Amy said after a long time. "If you did, we'd never be able to make love in the tree house again."

"Are you saying yes?" Harry inquired, leaning forward slightly in his chair.

"Yes," she replied, and then there were more tears. Happy ones, silvery in the candlelight.

Once again, Harry kept himself from shouting for joy, but just barely. He paid the check and, after the waiter had pulled back Amy's chair, helped her into her wrap. When they reached the waiting limousine, he opened the door for her and gave the driver very rational directions.

It was only when they reached the privacy of their hotel suite that he put his hands on either side of

Amy's slender waist, hoisted her over one shoulder and carried her to bed for a proper celebration.

In the morning Amy and Harry went shopping. She bought a toy koala bear for Ashley and a Crocodile Dundee hat for Oliver, and Harry bought an engagement ring.

He put it on her finger that afternoon, on board the jet, with Australia falling away behind them. Amy was pretty certain she could have flown home without an airplane, she was so happy.

Twenty-six hours later, they touched down in Seattle. Harry drove her home in his van.

"You're going to need some time to recuperate," he said, when they were standing in her kitchen. "I have some business to take care of in New York, but I'll call you when I get back."

Jealousy flared in Amy's heart, but she was too tired from all that traveling and lovemaking to nurture the flame. If she was going to love Harry, then she had to trust him as well.

"I love you," she said.

He kissed her, weakening her knees and causing her heart to catch. "And I love you," he replied, his voice a low rumble.

The first thing Amy did was call the number in Kansas that Louise had given her. She talked to both Oliver and Ashley, who were having a grand time at the reunion, but said nothing about her own trip or the wedding awaiting her in the future. Those were subjects she wanted to bring up in person.

"We'll be home next Tuesday, according to Grampa," Ashley said. "I'm bringing you something really neat."

Amy smiled, picturing an ashtray in the shape of Kansas or maybe a plate bearing a painting of the state bird. "I'll be looking forward to that," she said.

After saying goodbye, Amy immediately dialed her friend Debbie. She would listen to the messages on her answering machine later.

"What do you *mean,* you went to Australia with Harry Griffith?" Debbie demanded, the moment the receptionist at the clinic put Amy through to her office.

Amy smiled, perched on the edge of her desk and wrapped the phone cord idly around one finger. "He asked me to marry him," she said. "And I said yes."

Debbie gave a delighted cry, then apparently had second thoughts. "Wait a minute. You don't know him all that well."

"I know him as well as I need to," Amy replied quietly. "And what happened to all those lectures you were handing out before I left? I think the general theme was, 'Amy, you've got to put your past behind you and get on with your life.'"

Debbie sighed. "It sounded good in theory. Do you love this guy?"

"With all my heart."

"I'm coming right over. We'll go out for pizza and talk this through—"

"I'm not going anywhere," Amy sighed. "Not tonight. I just traveled from one hemisphere to another and I'm exhausted. I'm planning to have some soup, take a bath and crawl into bed."

"All right, we'll talk tomorrow, then," Debbie said breathlessly. "You're not going to live in Australia, are you?"

"Only part of the year," Amy answered, half yawning the words. "Goodbye, Debbie."

Before her friend could protest, Amy hung up.

She could barely see to heat soup, but she knew she needed nourishment, so she made herself a bowl of chicken and stars. After eating about half of the impromptu meal, Amy stumbled upstairs, had the bath she'd promised herself, put on a cotton nightshirt and fell into bed.

"It's about time you got home," commented a disapproving male voice.

Amy's eyes flew open, and she sat bolt upright in bed, reaching feverishly for the lamp switch. The subsequent burst of lights showed Tyler standing at the foot of the bed, one foot balanced on the antique blanket chest.

The fact that this had happened before did nothing to ease the shock. In fact, by that time Amy had half convinced herself that she'd never seen Tyler's ghost at all.

"What are you doing here?" she managed, staring at him, blinking hard and then staring again.

Tyler shoved one hand through his curly brown hair and sighed. "I used to live here, remember? I used to live, period."

Amy tossed back the covers, meaning to scramble over to Tyler and see if she could pass her hand through him, like a projection from her father-in-law's old eight-millimeter movie camera.

But Ty stepped back, and the expression on his face, though a benevolent one, was unmistakably a warning. "Don't try to touch me, Amy," he said. "It dissipates my energy."

Kneeling in the middle of the bed that had once been theirs, Amy covered her face with both hands. "This is insane. *I'm* insane!"

"I told you before," Tyler sighed, "you're perfectly all right. Where have you been for the past week?"

Amy lowered her hands. "You don't know? That's weird. I thought you knew all, saw all."

"I'm confined to a certain area," Tyler explained somewhat impatiently. "And my time is running out. Where were you, Amy? And where are the kids?"

"Ashley and Oliver are in Kansas, with your parents," she answered, worried. "And I was in Australia, with Harry Griffith. What do you mean, your time is running out?"

Tyler turned away for a moment.

"Ty?"

He held up one hand. "It's okay, Amy. I knew you and Harry were going to hit it off—it was meant to be—but it's still a little hard to let go."

Amy's throat tightened, and her eyes filled with tears. "You're telling me. Losing you was the worst thing that ever happened to me, Ty. If I could have held on to you even a moment longer, I would have."

When he turned to face her again, his eyes were suspiciously bright. He started to say something, then stopped himself.

Amy drew a deep breath and held it for a moment, struggling to regain her composure. She adored Harry, and she knew marrying him was the right thing to do, but Tyler had been her first love, the father of her children, and saying goodbye to him would not be easy.

"Will I see you again—someday?" she asked, clasping her hands together in her lap.

"Our paths may cross at some point," he answered gruffly. "Whether or not we'll recognize each other is another question. Be happy, Spud."

He started to fade.

"Tyler!" Amy cried. "Don't go!"

Between one instant and the next, however, Tyler disappeared completely.

Amy switched out the lamp and cried herself to sleep, and when Harry called the next morning, her throat was scratchy and she felt as though she hadn't slept in a week. He told her he'd be back the following day, and that he loved her, but that was all Amy could remember of the conversation.

"I saw Tyler again last night," she told Debbie, when the two of them met for pizza and salad at a restaurant near the clinic.

Debbie took the announcement in stride, just as she had before. "Part of the grieving process, I'm sure."

"He was really there!" Amy insisted.

"I believe that you believe that," Debbie replied. "Tyler came to say goodbye, didn't he?"

Amy couldn't deny that. She knew her grudging nod only confirmed her friend's theory that Tyler was some kind of subconscious manifestation.

"Do you still love him?" Debbie uttered the question subtly, spearing a cherry tomato from her salad bowl while she spoke.

"Tyler?" Amy searched her heart, and found a deep, sweet sadness there. "Not in the same way as before," she confessed, her voice barely audible.

"Separation complete," Debbie said.

"You think I'm crazy."

"I think you're a perfectly normal woman who loved her first husband to distraction. But you're young and you're healthy and now you care for somebody else."

Amy dried her eyes with a wadded napkin and sniffled. "Last night, you weren't quite so blithe about it."

"I was having a personal conflict," Debbie said matter-of-factly, every inch the professional. "You're my best friend, and I don't exactly relish the idea of seeing you move to Australia."

"I told you, it will only be for half the year."

"I'm not used to having to wait six months for a lunch date, Amy," Debbie pointed out. "This is going to create a serious gap in my social life. How do you think the kids will react to the news? And Tyler's parents?"

Amy sighed. "Ashley and Oliver adore Harry," she said. "The Ryans like him, too, of course, but I'm not sure how they're going to feel about being separated from their grandchildren for such long periods."

"They could visit," Debbie said practically.

"So could you," Amy pointed out.

Debbie beamed. "You're right. Will you introduce me to Paul Hogan?"

"Why not?" Amy teased with a shrug. "I'll probably know everybody in Australia on a first-name basis."

Later, Amy stopped by the supermarket to buy milk, fresh vegetables, cat food and a magazine. When she arrived home, Mrs. Ingallstadt was there, feeding Rumpel.

"My goodness, you scared me!" the old woman said, laying one plump hand to her heart.

Amy smiled. "I'm sorry. I should have called, but I was so tired when I got home yesterday."

"That's all right, dear," Mrs. Ingallstadt said kindly. "You've got a very good cat here, though it seems to me the poor creature is a little on the jumpy side."

Amy had been taking groceries from the canvas shopping bag she always brought to the store with her, but she stopped. Something in Mrs. Ingallstadt's tone had put all her senses on the alert. "Jumpy?"

"Cats are generally unflappable, you know," the neighbor explained. "But every time I came over, she flung herself into my arms and meowed like there was no tomorrow. I could hardly get her to settle down to eat.''

If the cat had seen Tyler, that would prove he was real and not a delusion. Wouldn't it?

''Maybe she saw a ghost,'' Amy said with a nervous giggle.

Mrs. Ingallstadt didn't smile. ''I used to see my Walter sometimes—after he was gone, I mean.''

Amy no longer made any pretense of being interested in the groceries. ''Really? What was he doing?''

The old lady chuckled fondly. ''Cleaning out the bird bath in the backyard,'' she said. ''I saw him on and off for about three years, I guess. Then, once I knew I could make my way alone, he stopped paying me visits.''

Pulling back a chair, Amy sank into it. ''Do you think you really saw Walter, or was it just your imagination?''

''Oh, I think I really saw him,'' Mrs. Ingallstadt said confidently. ''I may be old, but I know when I'm daydreaming. Walter was as real as you are.''

Amy wanted to laugh and cry, both at once. Her emotions were so tangled she couldn't begin to sort them out. ''Why do you think he came back?'' she ventured after a few moments.

Mrs. Ingallstadt smiled. ''He was looking after me the only way he could,'' she said. ''Walter always promised he'd stand by me, no matter what.'' She approached and laid a hand on Amy's shoulder. ''Are you all right, dear? You look a little peaky.''

Amy couldn't tell her neighbor and friend about seeing Tyler, not then at least. But she was overjoyed to know she wasn't the only one who'd had such an experience.

That night she made herself a salad, ate and went to bed early.

In the middle of the morning, Harry arrived, carrying an enormous bag full of rose petals. He poured the cloud of white softness onto the living-room floor, laid Amy on top of them and made slow, exacting love to her.

While she was caught up in the last, fevered stages of response, he gently squeezed her bottom and spoke to her in low, soothing words.

She was drenched with perspiration when she finally lay still, caressing Harry's strong shoulders while he strained upon her and finally spilled his passion.

"I have a bed, you know," she said much later, when he was lying with his head on her breast. She entangled her finger in an ebony curl as she spoke.

He raised up far enough to look her in the eye. "Tyler's bed," he pointed out.

"Ty would approve of our getting married," Amy said. She was certain of that, since Tyler had told her so himself.

"I know," Harry agreed, caressing her intimately. "But a man's bed is sacred."

Amy gasped as his finger slid inside her. His thumb, meanwhile, was making slow revolutions of its own.

She used the last of her strength to rebel, to bait him. "You mean, if you—died—I couldn't bring my third husband to the tree house?"

Harry bent to nibble at a breast that was still wet from previous forays of his tongue. "Not a chance. I'd haunt you."

Amy's last coherent thought was *It wouldn't be the first time that had happened.*

Hours later, when she and Harry were eating homemade spaghetti in Amy's kitchen, she said boldly, "I want you to stay here tonight."

The swift flatness of Harry's answer surprised her. "No."

"We could sleep in the guest room," Amy said reasonably. She'd been alone for two years, and now that she had someone to share her life again, she didn't want to sleep solo.

Harry shook his head. "Tyler's house," he said.

Amy was frightened, although she couldn't have explained the sensation. "That didn't stop you from making love to me in the middle of the living room," she pointed out in what she hoped was an even voice.

"I was desperate," Harry replied. "We'd been apart."

"I don't believe this!"

"Believe it. I love you, Amy, and I'm convinced Tyler would be happy about our being together. But he was one of my best friends and making love to his widow, under *his* roof, is not my idea of a fitting memorial."

Now Amy understood why she was scared. Harry was going to think of Tyler every time they were intimate, and maybe it would get so it didn't matter where they were at the time.

"Suppose I told you I'd seen Tyler," she burst out, without thinking. "Suppose I said he'd *told* me you and I were going to be married and have two children!"

Harry pushed away his plate. "Then I'd say you weren't through grieving and the last thing you were ready for was a new relationship."

The room seemed to sway around Amy; she gripped the table's edge to steady herself.

"What's going on here?" she demanded. "Are you getting cold feet?"

"If anybody's entitled to ask what's going on, love, I am!" Harry roared, throwing down his napkin and shooting to his feet. "Are you over Tyler or not?"

Amy was stunned. Although she'd seen anger snapping in Harry's blue eyes, she'd never heard him yell before. She'd never even *imagined* him yelling. "Yes, I'm over him," she said in a small, stricken voice.

"But you've seen him?"

Amy wanted to say no, but she couldn't lie. Not to Harry. So she didn't say anything at all.

Harry bent and kissed her angrily on the mouth. Amy didn't know if he was mad at her or himself.

She followed him to the front door and stood on the step, watching him storm down the walk.

"I love you, Harry," she called after him.

"I love you!" he shouted back.

That weekend, he and Amy went to Vashon Island together, to get the lighthouse ready for occupancy. They washed windows and walls and bathtubs all day Saturday, and made love in front of the fireplace most of the night. On Sunday they chose furniture from the showroom of an exclusive Seattle department store.

Sunday evening, Amy broiled steaks for dinner, and they ate at the picnic table in her backyard.

She wanted to ask Harry to stay, but she didn't because she knew he'd say no. He'd been his old self at the lighthouse, but once they were back in Seattle, he acted as though Tyler were looking over his shoulder.

They indulged in a passionate kiss, there in the backyard, and Harry helped Amy carry the debris from their meal into the house. He rinsed their plates and utensils, and she loaded the dishwasher.

When that was done, Harry said good-night, promised to call the next day and left.

Amy was brewing a cup of decaf when Tyler put in another one of his appearances.

This time he was sitting at the kitchen table, his chin propped in one hand.

Amy set the coffee aside so she wouldn't spill it.

"I'm not supposed to be here, actually."

"Then why—?"

"You're pregnant," he said, looking and sounding as pleased as if he'd accomplished the deed himself. "I just thought you might like to know that."

Instinctively, Amy put both hands to her flat stomach. "I can't be pregnant," she said. "I took precautions."

"Precautions don't mean diddly where The Plan is concerned," Tyler replied blithely. "It's a girl. Dark hair, blue eyes. She'd going to run Harry's company someday."

Amy felt dizzy. She'd barely come to terms with her feelings for Harry as it was.

"Tyler, I'm imagining you. You're not here and I'm not seeing you!"

"I hope not," observed a third voice.

Amy whirled to find Harry standing in the kitchen doorway. The expression in his eyes was bleak, resigned, and Amy knew he couldn't see Tyler.

"Do something!" Amy ordered Tyler frantically. "Show yourself, make a sound, tip over the table—something!"

"It's no use, Spud," Tyler said with a philosophical sigh. "Nobody can see or hear me but you. And the cat, of course. To show myself to Harry would take so much energy that I'd probably short out or something."

Amy turned to Harry. "He's really here," she cried. "Harry, I swear I'm not having delusions—Tyler is *right here!*"

Harry looked sad. "It's obvious that you're not ready for a new marriage, Amy." He collected his sweater, which he'd left draped over the back of a chair. "I'll call you sometime."

"Harry!"

"Now I know why they told me not to come back," Tyler muttered.

"Oh, shut up!" Amy yelled. She'd finally found happiness, and it was walking out the door.

Harry paused on the front step. "Do you want me to call your doctor or something?" he asked.

Amy bit her lower lip, held back all the fevered denials and angry defenses that rushed into her throat. It was too late now, Harry had heard her talking to someone he couldn't see or hear, and he thought she was in the midst of some emotional crisis.

"I'll be fine," she managed to say.

Harry got into his van, closed the door and drove away.

The next day Ashley and Oliver returned from their trip, bearing gifts from every tacky souvenir shop between Seattle and Topeka, or so it seemed. Amy was delighted to see them; they were, at the moment, her only viable reasons for not going crazy.

"That's a pretty ring," Oliver told her that night, when he'd had his bath and his story, and she was tucking him into bed.

Amy looked at the diamond engagement ring she would have to return and sighed. "It is pretty, isn't it?" she said sadly. "I only borrowed it, though."

"I missed you a whole bunch, Mom," Oliver confided. "A couple of times I even thought I might cry." He whispered the final word, lest it fall on enemy ears. Ashley's, for instance.

Amy kissed her son on the forehead. "I missed you a whole bunch, too, and I *did* cry," she said.

"I know," Oliver replied. "Your eyes are all red and swelly, like they used to be after Dad died."

"I've got some problems," she told the child honestly, "but I'll work them out, so I don't want you to worry, all right?"

"All right," Oliver agreed, closing his eyes and settling into his pillow with a sigh. "'Night, Mom."

Amy went on to Ashley's room. Her daughter was sitting up in bed, busy writing in her diary.

"I guess that trip to Kansas must have been pretty exciting," Amy said gently, standing near Ashley's ruffly, stuffed-animal-mounded bed.

"It was," Ashley beamed, "but I'm glad I'm home. What did you do while we were gone, Mom?"

Amy kissed the little girl's warm cheek. "That's a long story, baby," she answered gently. "But someday I'll tell you all about it."

She switched out Ashley's light and left the room, and in the hallway Amy touched her stomach again, wondering.

If she was about to present Ashley and Oliver with a little sister, as Tyler claimed, she'd be doing that explaining sooner rather than later.

Eight

Amy waited a full week for Harry to reach out and touch someone—namely, her. When he didn't, she tracked him down by calling the Ryans and asking for his office address and telephone number.

After summoning Mrs. Ingallstadt to look after the kids, Amy jumped into her car and set out for downtown Seattle.

Harry's investment firm was housed in one of the swanky, renovated buildings overlooking Elliott Bay. Clutching her courage as tightly as she clutched the handle of her purse, Amy took an elevator to the nineteenth floor.

A pretty receptionist greeted her from behind a tastefully designed desk when she entered the suite, and Amy felt another sting of envy. She was also more than a little nettled by the fact that she'd been going to marry the man and yet had had to call her former in-laws to find out where his office was located.

"I'd like to see Mr. Griffith, please."

The receptionist smiled. "I'll see if he's available. Your name?"

Amy swallowed, feeling at once foolish and belligerent. "Amy Ryan."

An exchange over the intercom followed, though Amy could only hear the receptionist's side.

"Go right in," the girl said, gesturing toward a heavy pair of mahogany doors.

Amy's bravado flagged a little, but she lifted her chin and squared her shoulders and walked boldly into Harry's inner office, closing the door behind her.

Harry sat behind an imposing library table desk, an antique from the looks of it, and he was as handsome as ever. His ebony hair gleamed in the subdued light coming in through elegantly shuttered windows, and he had taken off his coat to reveal a tailored white shirt and a gray silk brocade vest.

"Amy," he said. He hesitated before standing, just long enough to rouse Amy's ire.

Eyes flashing, she stormed over to one of the sumptuous leather chairs facing his desk and sat down, practically flinging her purse to the floor.

"I haven't had a decent night's sleep in a whole week!" she announced.

One corner of Harry's mouth tilted slightly upward, but he didn't exactly smile. Which was a damn good thing, Amy figured, because she was in no mood to be patronized.

"Nor have I," he replied in a husky voice. Sinking back to his chair, he made a steeple with his index fingers and propped them under his chin.

Amy's pride was in tatters, but her temper sustained her. "If you want your ring back," she challenged, "that's just tough. I'm keeping it!"

Harry sighed. "It wouldn't fit me, anyway," he retorted quietly.

Amy rushed on, just as though he hadn't spoken. "And the reason I'm not giving it back is because I still love you," she blurted out, "and I think what we have together is too special to throw away!"

He rose from the chair again to stand at one of the windows, his back to Amy. "To have you for my own and then lose you," he said, "would be a thousand times worse than never having you at all."

She felt the wrench of his words to the very core of her soul, and before she realized what she was doing, she went to him and laid her cheek against his back.

"Harry, what if we visited my friend Debbie—she's a psychologist, and she could reassure you that I'm not crazy—"

He turned and took her shoulders gently in his hands. "I never said you were crazy, love. I said you needed some time to work things through. Having me around would only complicate the process."

Amy couldn't resist; she laid her hands against his smooth-shaven, Aramis-scented cheeks. "Okay, we don't have to get married next week or next month. But I want you in my life, Harry."

Harry sighed, pulled Amy close and propped his chin on the top of her head. She was practically drunk on the strength and substance and fragrance of him.

"You didn't say you needed me," he pointed out, after an interval of sweet, poignant silence.

Amy laughed, even though there were tears in her eyes. "It's not fashionable for a woman to say she needs a man. I could end up with people picketing in front of my house."

Harry kissed her forehead. "Well, I don't give a damn about fashion or any of that other rot," he said. "I'm perfectly willing to admit it, Amy—I need you, even if it's only to be my friend."

She drew back in his arms, feeling as if he'd given her a kidney punch. "Your—friend?"

He cupped her chin in his hand. "Yes, Amy, your friend. Things got too hot, too fast between us. I should have known better."

Amy swallowed, feeling wretched. She wanted Harry's friendship, of course, but she also desired him as a lover. The idea of never making love in a tree house again, or on a bed of rose petals, was a desolate one. "What do you mean, you should have known better?"

Harry smoothed her hair back from her cheek, and his smile was infinitely sad. "You're still grieving for Tyler, and I guess I am, too. It's impossible to tell whether what we feel for each other is real."

"Harry—"

He traced the outline of her mouth with one index finger. "Shh. We'll be mates, you and I. No need to complicate that with sex and marriage and all that."

Amy's cheeks were warm with color. "Were you trifling with me before?" she demanded.

He chuckled. "*Trifling?* You've been reading too many Victorian novels, Amy." He paused, seeing her ire, and cleared his throat. "It's because I love you," he concluded solemnly, "that I refuse to take further advantage of your emotional state."

She stepped back, because being so close to Harry made her ache in ways that would not be relieved in the foreseeable future. "I guess that's better than nothing," she concluded, speaking more to herself than to Harry. She turned and moved toward the door, as if in a daze.

Amy wondered how she was supposed to feel now. Happy? Sad?

She hadn't lost Harry exactly, but she hadn't really won him back, either. They were going to be *friends*.

Instead of going straight home, Amy drove across the Mercer Island bridge and made her way to her in-laws' gracious Tudor-style house. Louise met her at the door with a joyful hug.

"I'm relieved to see you're still speaking to me!" The older woman laughed. "After I let Ashley and Oliver buy you that awful Kansas ashtray, I thought your affection might cool a little."

They were in Louise's living room, about to have tea in delicate china cups that had belonged to Tyler's great-grandmother, before the older woman's expression turned serious.

"That's a very nice suntan you have," Louise said. "You didn't get that in Seattle."

Amy cleared her throat and looked away for a moment. Tyler was gone and she was an adult, free to do as she chose, but Amy still felt as though she were confessing to adultery. "While you and John and the kids were in Kansas," she finally said, "I went to Australia. With Harry Griffith."

Louise's smile was thoughtful, speculative, but not condemning. "I see."

Suddenly, without warning, Amy began to cry. She snuffled, and when Louise presented her with a box of tissue, blew her nose industriously.

"I take it you're in love with our Harry," Louise said with no little satisfaction. "Well, I think that's wonderful!"

Amy plucked a fresh batch of tissues from the box and blotted her mascara-stained cheeks. "You do?"

"Of course I do," Louise replied, reaching out to pat her daughter-in-law's hand. "You've been alone too long. All the better that it's Harry you've taken up with—for all practical intents and purposes, you'll still be our daughter-in-law."

"He wants to be my friend," Amy informed her gloomily. "He thinks I'm not ready for a new relationship."

"What gave him that idea?" Louise inquired in a calm tone, pouring more tea for herself and Amy.

Amy fidgeted in her chair. "It's—well—I just don't know how to tell you this!"

"How about just opening your mouth and spitting it right out?" Louise prompted matter-of-factly. She'd always been a proponent of the direct approach.

"I've seen Tyler—since he died, I mean. Several times."

To her credit, Louise didn't scream and run. She just drew her beautifully shaped eyebrows together for a moment in an elegant frown, then replied, "Oh, dear. I don't think that's very usual."

Amy shook her head miserably. "No, it isn't. But my neighbor used to see her late husband cleaning the bird bath, and Debbie says I'm not dealing with a ghost at all, but some projection from my deeper mind."

"Hmm," said Louise.

"Anyway," Amy went on, "Harry happened to walk in on one of my conversations with Tyler and now he thinks I haven't adjusted. For a whole week I didn't see Harry, and he didn't call. Now he wants to be—" she began to cry again "—*buddies*."

"I think things will work out, dear. You and Harry just need a little time, that's all."

"You don't think I'm weird for seeing Tyler?"

Louise smiled sadly and shook her head. "There were times when I thought I caught a glimpse of him myself, just out of the corner of my eye. When you love someone, they leave a lasting imprint on your world."

Amy wanted to tell Louise there might be a baby, a dark-haired, blue-eyed girl who would one day run Harry's empire, but she figured she'd done enough soul baring for one day. Besides, if Tyler was really a figment of her imagination, then the baby was nothing more than wishful thinking.

"You've been a big help," Amy said, gathering up what seemed like a square acre of crumpled tissue and carrying it to the wastebasket.

"Why don't you bring the kids over for dinner tonight?" Louise said eagerly. "I'll be all alone if you don't come."

Assuming her father-in-law was out of town playing golf or overseeing some investment property he and Louise owned in the eastern part of the state, Amy didn't question Louise's statement. "Sure," she said. "Why not?"

"See you at seven," Louise replied, "and dress pretty."

When Amy returned to Mercer Island that evening, wearing her green suede and silk jumpsuit with a lightweight white jacket, she was surprised to find Harry's van parked in the Ryans' driveway.

"Harry's here!" Oliver crowed, bounding out of the car a second after Amy had brought it to a stop.

Ashley was more circumspect, but Amy could see that her daughter was just as pleased.

As for Amy, well, her mother-in-law's final words were echoing in her ears. *Dress pretty.*

"I should have known you were up to something," Amy accused pleasantly, when Louise answered the door. "Did you call him up the minute I agreed to come to dinner?"

After hugging their grandmother, Oliver and Ashley rushed inside in search of Harry.

"As a matter of fact, yes," Louise answered.

When Harry stepped into the entryway, wearing gray slacks and a blue summer sweater, Amy could have sworn the earth backtracked on its axis for a few degrees before plunging forward again.

"Hello, Amy."

She resisted an urge to smooth her hair and her jacket. "Hello," she replied.

"I'll just leave the two of you to chat while I go and put the chicken on the grill," Louise announced busily. A moment later she was gone.

Amy just stood there, as embarrassed as if she'd crashed a private party. Ashley and Oliver appeared behind Harry, anxious for his attention.

Harry held his hands out to his sides, and Ashley and Oliver each took one, on cue. "We're going for a walk down by the water. Want to go along?"

Since her emotions were as raw as an exposed nerve, Amy opted out. "I'll stay here and help Louise with the chicken," she said.

Harry's ink-blue eyes swept over her once, in a way that used to precede a session of lovemaking. "You're not exactly dressed for barbecuing, but I guess that's your choice."

Having made this cryptic pronouncement, Harry turned and walked back through the big house, taking Amy's children with him.

Amy took an alternate route to the big deck overlooking the water and found Louise there, busily brushing her special sauce onto the chicken pieces she'd already arranged on the grill.

The elder Mrs. Ryan looked at her daughter-in-law quizzically. "Didn't you want to join Harry and the children on their walk?"

"I think Ashley and Oliver need to have him to themselves for a little while," Amy answered.

Louise smiled, watching with a wistful expression in her eyes as the three figures moved down the verdant hillside behind the house. "Tyler was a good father," she said. "It's not surprising that his children miss the presence of a man."

"They have their grandfathers and their uncles," Amy pointed out.

"That's not quite the same," Louise said, meeting Amy's eyes, "and we both know it. Children need a man who not only loves them, but loves their mother as well. And Harry loves you passionately."

Amy went to the deck railing, helpless to turn away, and stood watching, listening to her children's laughter on the evening breeze. Watching Harry and shamelessly wanting him.

"Harry's not sure what he feels," Amy mused. "He told me that himself. He thinks we need time."

"Harry may very well not be sure what he feels," Louise replied without hesitation, "but he's wildly in love with you. He might as well have the fact tattooed on his forehead.''

Amy smiled at that image, though she felt more like crying. It seemed to her, in her present fragile mood, that love should be simpler than it was. With Tyler, romance had been as natural as breathing, and their relationship had progressed without a hitch.

Finally remembering her original plan to help with the chicken, Amy turned and started toward the grill.

''Stay back,'' Louise warned, brandishing her barbecue fork. ''You're not dressed for this.''

The sun was starting to dip behind the horizon when Harry, Ashley and Oliver climbed the wooden stairs behind the house to join the small party on the deck. Amy's heart started thumping painfully the minute Harry was within a dozen feet of her, and she wondered how on earth she was ever going to stand just being his friend.

Ashley and Oliver chattered non-stop, all through dinner, and Amy was relieved because that saved her from having to make conversation. The moment the meal was over, however, Louise enlisted the kids to help clear away the dishes, leaving Amy and Harry alone at the redwood picnic table Ty and his father had built one long-ago summer.

''I'm sorry,'' Amy said. She gazed at the city lights and their aura of stars because she still wasn't bold enough to look straight at Harry. ''Louise seems to be throwing us together.''

Their knees touched under the table, and Harry drew back as if he'd been burned. "She's a matchmaker at heart."

Amy swallowed. She'd made love with this man in a tree house, for heaven's sake, not to mention the bedroom of a fancy jet and on her own living-room floor. For all of that, she felt nervous with him, vulnerable and shy.

"Thank you for paying so much attention to the kids," she choked out. "They miss having a man around."

"It isn't an act of charity, Amy," Harry said quietly. She sensed that he was about to take her hand, but when she looked, he withdrew. "I love kids. I've always wanted a whole houseful of my own."

Amy considered telling him she might be pregnant, but decided against it. Her crazy confessions had gotten her into enough trouble. Besides, as much as she loved Harry, as much as she yearned to share her life with him, she didn't want him to marry her as a point of honor. When Harry became her husband, it had to be by his own choice, not by coercion.

"Let's go in," he said, when the silence grew long and awkward. "It's getting chilly."

"I noticed," Amy replied ruefully, but she wasn't talking about the weather.

For the next month Amy saw Harry only when she went to dinner at her in-laws' house, or when he could be sure Ashley and Oliver would be around to act as chaperons.

Right after Labor Day, school started, and Amy told herself it was time to start concentrating on her real estate deals again. Instead of putting on a power suit and going out to meet with a potential client, however, she jumped into the car and headed for the nearest drugstore the minute the school bus turned the corner.

In the end, though, Amy didn't have the nerve to go into that familiar neighborhood establishment and buy what she needed. She drove on until she found another one, where the proprietors were strangers.

Even then, Amy wore sunglasses and a big hat while making her purchase.

At home again, she tore open the box and rushed into the downstairs bathroom to perform the pregnancy test.

The process took twenty minutes, and the results were positive.

Amy sat on the edge of the bathtub, unable to decide whether she should mourn or celebrate. Her relationship with Harry was clearly over, except for his playing doting uncle to the kids, and nobody knew better than Amy did how hard it was to raise a child alone.

On the other hand, she had wanted another baby for a long time. In fact, she and Tyler had planned to have at least two more little ones—until fate intervened.

Amy needed desperately to talk to someone. After throwing away the paraphernalia from her test and washing her hands, she wandered out into the living room.

"Tyler?"

Nothing.

Struck by another impulse, Amy brushed her hair, applied fresh lip gloss and snatched up her purse and keys. Within minutes she was on the road again.

When she reached the cemetery where Tyler had been buried, she parked the car and sat behind the wheel for a while, struggling to contain her emotions.

Finally she walked up the hill to Tyler's grave. His grandparents and another Ryan son who'd died in childhood shared the well-maintained plot.

After looking around carefully and seeing nobody but a gardener off in the distance, Amy touched Tyler's marble headstone lovingly, then sat down on a nearby bench.

Five minutes passed, then ten, then fifteen. Amy wiped away a tear with the back of one hand.

"Oh, Ty, what am I going to do? You were right about the baby—I'm pregnant, and Harry's going to know the child is his. He'll insist on doing the honorable thing, and we'll have one of those terrible, grudging marriages—"

A breeze, warm because it was still early in September, ruffled the leaves of the trees and wafted through Amy's hair.

"Tyler, you started all this," Amy went on. "You've got to help me. You've got to tell me what to do."

There was no answer, and yet Amy thought she could sense Tyler's presence. Maybe it was only a silly fancy.

"I'm open to suggestions!" Amy said, spreading her hands wide in a gesture of acceptance.

An older couple stopped to look at her, probably wondering if they should scream for help, then hurried on, hand in hand.

"You're no help at all!" Amy whispered, bending a little closer to the headstone so her voice wouldn't carry. But it did help to sit there, talking to Tyler. Only when she was driving away did Amy realize that she'd said a goodbye of her own, final and complete.

She just wished there were a way to convince Harry that she'd turned the corner, that she was ready to love him with her whole heart. As for her body, well, that was *more* than ready to love Harry.

"Harry's living at the lighthouse now," Tyler's sister, Charlotte, announced that night, when she came to have supper with Amy and the kids.

Amy thought of the child growing within her and ached to share the news, but, much as she dreaded telling Harry, she knew he had to be the first to know.

"Oh?" Amy tried to sound unconcerned as she assembled a salad. "Is he dating anybody?"

Charlotte shook her head. "You're not fooling me with the casual act, Amy. You can hardly keep your hands off the man. What's going on between you two, anyway?"

"I wish I knew," Amy sighed. "He thinks I'm not over Tyler." She gazed out the kitchen window at the lilacs, withered now with the coming of fall, and felt sad because Ty had loved them so much.

Charlotte shrugged. "It's Friday," she said. "Why don't you go out to the lighthouse and talk things over with Harry? I'll stay here and look after the kids."

"I couldn't—"

"Why not?"

"It would be too forward."

Charlotte rolled her eyes. "Amy, you're not in junior high school. And you love this guy, don't you?"

Amy nodded. "I always thought it could only happen once."

"Well, don't blow it," Charlotte hissed happily. "Go! Get out of here!"

"What if he's with someone else?" Amy whispered. "I'd die."

"He won't be," Charlotte replied in a confident tone of voice, "but if you insist on being civilized, call first."

"No," Amy said resolutely. But when Charlotte and the kids were eating, she found she couldn't choke down a bite of the special eggplant dish she'd made.

Finally she went into the den and closed the door.

She didn't have to call information, or Louise, for Harry's new number. It was branded on her mind in steaming digits.

He answered on the third ring, with a gravelly and somewhat impatient "Hello?"

Amy wondered despairingly if she'd pulled him away from a glass of wine, a crackling fire and a willing woman. "Hello," she finally managed to say.

"Amy?" Her name echoed with alarm. "Are you all right? Has something happened to one of the kids?"

She cleared her throat. "No," she said as quickly as possible. "I mean, yes, I'm all right, and no, nothing has happened to Ashley or Oliver. I just...wanted to talk with you."

He was silent, waiting for her to go on, but she couldn't tell whether it was a receptive silence or an impatient, angry one.

"Do you think I could come out there? There's a ferry in half an hour, and I can catch it if I hurry."

It was agony, waiting for his answer. "All right," he finally said, and again, his tone betrayed none of his emotions.

Amy dropped her toothbrush into her purse, grabbed her coat and gave Charlotte the okay sign from the dining-room doorway.

After saying good-bye to Ashley and Oliver, carefully avoiding any explanation of her destination the whole while, Amy rushed out to her car.

She made the ferry with only seconds to spare.

Finding the lighthouse, once she reached the island, was easy. The structure's giant electric lamp was shining in the darkness, guiding her.

When she pulled up in front of Harry's spectacular house, he came out to meet her, his blue eyes searching her face worriedly in the glow from above. He took her arm and shuffled her inside and across a glistening hardwood floor to the fireplace.

"What's this about?" Harry asked. "Are you all right?"

Amy could no longer carry the burden alone, and besides, her secret was going to be obvious enough in the months to come. She needed to tell Debbie and Louise and Charlotte, in order to enlist their support, and she couldn't do that until Harry knew.

"I'm going to have a baby," she said bluntly.

Harry's mouth dropped open. "I thought... ?"

"That I was protected? So did I. But sometimes babies just decide they're going to be born, no matter what."

His hands closed on her shoulders, firmly but with a gentleness that touched her heart. He pressed her into the big leather chair they'd picked out together, that happy day before things had fallen apart.

"I'm not sick, Harry," Amy pointed out practically. "Just pregnant."

"When?" He croaked the word, paused to clear his throat, and started again. "When will the little nipper be joining us?"

"In the spring," Amy answered, wishing there truly could be an *us*.

Harry was completely beside himself. He paced and ran one hand through his usually impeccable hair, and Amy would have laughed if the situation hadn't had such a serious side.

She knew she was about to get everything she wanted, for all the wrong reasons. And those reasons might well poison her relationship with this man forever. He'd soon view her the same way he'd seen Madeline—as a manipulator and a schemer.

"We'll have to be married right away," he said.

"No," Amy replied. "We can't get married."

Harry was quietly outraged. "Then what the hell are we going to do? You're not going to bring *my* child into this world with no claim to his rightful name! And don't suggest living together, because that wouldn't be good for Ashley and Oliver."

"I wasn't going to suggest living together," Amy said. "I think we should just go on as we have been." *Even though it's torture,* she thought, *that's better than it would be to look into your eyes and see contempt, or boredom, or God help us both, hatred.*

He took her hand, pulled her easily to her feet. "I think I know how to convince you," he said. And then he slanted his mouth over hers for a commanding kiss, and Amy thought she'd faint with excitement and relief.

Nine

The fact that he knew better didn't keep Harry from making love to Amy. Nor did the realization that she was carrying his child; *that* only made her more attractive.

No, Harry could no more have turned away from her than a starving man could resist hot cornbread dripping with butter.

They didn't even get as far as the bed, but instead sank to the Persian rug on the hearth. Their clothes melted away and their tongues mated and then, suddenly, their bodies were engaged in the ancient struggle, twisting and writhing and colliding with sweet, fevered violence.

Arched beneath him, Amy threw her head back and gave a long, guttural cry. Tendrils of her hair clung to the moisture on her forehead and cheeks, and her eyes stared sightlessly past him, past the ceiling and the night sky.

Harry's own climax was fast approaching when he saw surprise in her features, felt her sated body come alive once more under his hips, heard her murmur with joyous desperation, "Oh, God, Harry, it's going to happen—again!"

Harry drove deep inside her, and she came apart in his arms, chattering senselessly, enfolding him in her strong, slender legs. A sound that was half sob and half shout of triumph tore itself from Harry's throat, and he stiffened upon Amy, surrendering what she demanded of him.

For several long moments, his body spasmed violently in response to her gentle conquering. Then he collapsed beside her on the rug in front of his fireplace.

"We'll be married as soon as we can get the license," he said a long time later, when he had regained enough strength to speak.

She shook her head, which had been resting placidly on his shoulder until that moment.

"No, Harry, we won't. I don't want it to be like this."

Harry swallowed a growl of frustration; this was no time to be macho. He was proud of the fact that he spoke so calmly. "Tell me what you want, Amy, and I'll give it to you."

She raised herself on one elbow, and the firelight bathed her satiny, naked flesh, making Harry want her all over again. "I want you to want me, for *me*. Not because I'm carrying your baby, not because you feel obliged to look after your good friend's widow, but because you're absolutely wild about me."

He raised her fingers to his lips and kissed the knuckles lightly, one by one. "I thought I just proved that."

"You just proved that you wanted *a woman*, Harry. I refuse to buy the delusion that someone else couldn't have satisfied you just as completely."

Harry sighed. God, but women were a frustrating lot, always attacking a man's pure logic with their reasonable implausibilities. The bloke who figured out what in the hell they really wanted would make millions.

"I love you," he said. "You know that."

She laid her head on his chest again and started making circular motions on his belly with one hand. If she kept that up, he'd be out of his mind in about five seconds. "I know we have good chemistry," she argued sweetly. "I also know that you were perfectly willing to end everything between us until you found out about the baby."

With another sigh, Harry shoved splayed fingers through his hair. "All right, rose petal, jump to whatever conclusions that might look comfortable. But add this to the list of things you know—I have rights where this child is concerned and I *will not* sacrifice them."

He felt her shiver in his arms, but when she executed her special vengeance, her hand was damnably strong and steady.

"Oh, God," he rasped, closing his eyes.

Amy was kissing her way down over his chest, his rib cage, his midriff. "Even prayer won't help you now, Harry Griffith." She purred the words, but not as a kitten would. Oh, no. This was a lioness.

Harry gave a strangled gasp of pleasure when she claimed him.

The next morning, Amy awakened in Harry's bed. She'd spent the night in heaven, but now, as she sat there alone, she returned to earth with a painful thump. Nothing had really been resolved, nothing had changed.

She sat bolt upright and looked wildly around for her clothes.

With perfect timing, Harry entered the room, carrying a tray with a coffee cup, a covered plate and a newspaper on it.

"Where are my things?" Amy demanded, embarrassed to remember how she'd behaved the night before. Merciful heavens, this man could turn her into a harlot with a touch or a single kiss.

He grinned, setting the tray across her lap. "What clothes?" he asked innocently.

"The ones I was wearing last night, when I arrived," Amy answered tightly. She wanted to spurn the food he'd brought, but she'd had a world-class workout and she was hungry. She lifted the lid from the covered plate and nibbled at a piece of fresh pineapple.

"Oh," Harry replied, in a tone of great revelation, standing back from the side of the bed, "you're speaking of the garments you tore off, in your eagerness to surrender yourself to me in front of the fireplace last night." He paused, rubbing his chin. "I'm afraid I burned them."

Amy's fork clattered to the tray. *"You burned them?"*

Harry nodded. "Essentially, rose petal, you're a prisoner of love. Unless you want to make the trip back to Seattle in the altogether, of course."

She narrowed her eyes. "You're making this up!"

"See for yourself," Harry said, gesturing toward the door leading to the living room. "Of course, I feel honor bound to tell you that you'll be taking a big chance, just walking past me. There's something about impending fatherhood that makes me—well—eager."

Color flooded Amy's face, but it was a blush of chagrin and not anger. She'd just realized that she didn't mind the prospect of being Harry's toy for a while, and that insight embarrassed her greatly.

"What are the conditions for my release?" she asked after sitting there for a long time, staring at Harry like a fool.

He raised an index finger. "Oh, there is only one. You'll have to become my wife."

Amy closed her eyes, took a deep breath and let it out again. With that she was calm. She wouldn't scream and yell.

She opened her eyes and her mouth at the same time, and when she did she found that Harry was gone.

Furiously Amy stuffed down the rest of her breakfast. Then, wrapping herself in the bedspread, she got up and started going through Harry's bureau drawers.

She put on a pair of his briefs in place of underpants, but he didn't have anything that could be adapted to serve as a bra. After adding tailored wool slacks, a cinched belt, a striped, button-down shirt, socks and a pair of loafers that flippity-flopped when she walked, Amy stormed defiantly into the living room.

"I'm leaving," she said.

A corner of Harry's mouth quivered, but he didn't laugh. He didn't even smile. He closed the book he'd been reading and rose from his chair. "How? I've hidden your car, not to mention your purse, and if you try to walk to the ferry terminal in my clothes, the police will probably pick you up and haul you off to some shelter."

Amy stomped one foot. "Harry, this isn't funny."

His blue eyes swept over her. "That's your opinion, rose petal. I think it's hilarious." Another sweep of his eyes left her feeling weak. "Come here," he said.

Although reason and pride dictated that she must stand her ground, instinct prevailed. Amy stepped out of the loafers and walked slowly across the room to Harry.

Methodically, he untucked the shirt she'd borrowed, then unfastened the belt buckle. The slacks fell straight to the floor, and Harry chuckled when he saw the briefs beneath.

Reaching smoothly, boldly inside the flap, he cupped her femininity in his hand, making a circular motion with his palm.

"Harry," she whimpered, helpless to twist away from him because he'd already made her need what he was doing to her.

"Open the shirt, Amy," he said. "I want to see your breasts."

She obeyed him, moving slowly and deliberately, like some creature under a spell. All the defiance she could come up with was "You can't make love to me in the living room in broad daylight, Harry."

"Watch me," he replied. Then, still caressing her, he plunged one finger deep inside her and, at the same moment, bent to take one of her nipples greedily into his mouth.

He brought her to the very edge of release, made her coast back to earth just short of satisfaction, then carried her high again.

Finally, sitting in his leather wing-back chair, he positioned Amy on his lap, facing him, her knees draped over the arms. She was transfixed when he took her, letting out a long, low, primitive cry of pure animal pleasure.

His hands gripping the quivering flesh of her hips, Harry rocked Amy back and forth until she was literally out of her mind with passion. He sucked her breasts, first one and then the other, while she shivered again and again and again.

Finally Harry climaxed, too, and she was allowed to sag forward against him, her forehead propped on his shoulder.

"You didn't really burn my clothes," she managed, after some time.

"Oh, yes I did," he replied. "Marry me."

Amy trembled, still filled with him, her legs still balanced over the arms of the chair. "No."

He took her to the master bath, bathed her languid body thoroughly in the big marble tub, then, in his room, placed her atop a bureau and had her again.

If Amy had told Harry she didn't want to make love, he would have respected her wishes and left her alone. The trouble was, he was very good at arousing her, and by the time he'd gone through all the steps, she was more than ready to cooperate.

Her responses this time were just as wild, just as violent, as before. Harry had opened some well of need inside her, some region of surrender that had never been reached before.

"Marry me," he said intractably, kissing her shoulder blades, when she finally stopped howling in raucous appeasement.

"Absolutely not," Amy gasped with the last of her defiance.

Harry began to massage her bottom with both hands, although he did not withdraw from her depths because he had somehow stopped himself on the brink of satisfaction and he was still hard inside her.

Slowly, rhythmically, he began to move—in, out, in, out.

Amy groaned and clutched the edges of the bureau. "Oh, no," she whimpered, feeling the treacherous pressure begin to build inside her. "Oh, Harry, don't make me—"

He did make her, though.

More than once.

"Harry," she said, much later, huddled in his bed again, with the covers pulled to her chin, "I have children. I must get back to them."

"Louise and Charlotte are looking after the nippers," Harry replied. Fresh from the shower, he was wearing a dark blue terry robe with a hood, and his dark hair, only partially dry, was combed.

"What did you tell Louise?" Amy wanted to know.

"That I've made you my love slave and she shouldn't look for you to return to the city anytime soon," Harry replied, turning to stand in front of the dresser mirror.

"You didn't!" Amy cried in mortified disbelief, her cheeks hot with humiliation.

"Sure I did," Harry answered. "But don't look for the sheriff to come and save you, rose petal. Louise thought being a plaything might do you some good."

Amy snatched up a pillow and flung it at him, missing by a wide margin. "She did not. Louise is a very modern woman. She would never approve of this!"

Harry picked up the pillow and hurled it back with deadly accuracy. "She also comes from a generation where women married the men who made them pregnant. She thinks I should keep you here until I've made you see reason."

Amy swallowed, no longer sure what to believe. It was no small irritation to her pride that she secretly loved this game Harry was playing with her, and even though she was exhausted, she could hardly wait to see where he would make love to her next.

"You're a bastard, Harry Griffith," she sulked.

"And you're a hot little number who needs to be taken on a regular basis."

Again, it was the truth in Harry's statement that made Amy so angry.

"I hate you!" she yelled.

"Mmm-hmm," he answered distractedly. "It's going to be a man-sized job keeping you properly pleasured. Of course, I'm—" he paused, cleared his throat "—up to the task."

Amy screamed in frustration. "Damn you, Harry, get me some clothes and take me home, right now!"

He wrapped her in a heavy bathrobe of navy velvet and led her out to the living room, where he settled her in a chair by the hearth, then built up the fire. He brought her food, fruit and bread, and a snifter of brandy, and for a while she thought Harry was beginning to see reason.

Instead, he was resting up for another round.

Once she'd eaten, he took her back to bed and made love to her again.

"Will you marry me?" Harry inquired implacably, when she was dangling from the edge of ecstatic madness.

"Yes!" Amy cried. "Oh, Harry—oh, God—*yes!*"

Her reward left her drenched with perspiration and weak from her own straining efforts.

Harry finished what he'd begun, and after a long time, he got up and found oil to rub into every inch of her skin. Finally, then, he allowed her to sleep.

The next day a judge arrived with a special license, and Louise, John and Charlotte appeared with the children. Louise had brought along a flowered sundress for Amy to wear, along with casual clothes, nightgowns and underwear for later.

"You're sure you're okay with this?" Amy asked her children, when the three of them were alone in one of Harry's guest rooms. She hadn't told them, of course, how Harry had burned her clothes and made love to her repeatedly. "You really want a stepfather?"

"We really want *Harry*," Ashley clarified.

"We're going to live in Australia, on an island!" Oliver crowed, hardly able to contain his enthusiasm at this good fortune. "Wow!"

Amy was looking forward to becoming Harry's wife, but she was also reluctant. She couldn't get past the idea that none of this would be happening if she hadn't told Harry she was expecting his baby.

The wedding was to be held in Harry's living room, that evening, by the light of a hundred candles. All the rest of Tyler's family came over for the occasion, and since Amy's father couldn't take enough time off from being a world-renowned surgeon to make the trip, John Ryan gave away the bride.

Oliver was to be the best man, Ashley the maid of honor.

Amy went to the master bedroom to be alone and gather her thoughts before the ceremony, and what she found there practically stopped her heart in midbeat.

In the middle of the bed, fragrant and lacy and totally impossible, lay an armload of white lilacs.

Mentally Amy searched the lighthouse grounds, and she found no lilacs. They couldn't have come from the mainland, either, because there had been a hard freeze the last week in August and all the flowers were gone.

Slowly, her eyes filling with happy tears, Amy approached the bed and lifted one of the lovely fronds into her hands. She was drawing in its unforgettable scent when she heard the door open.

Harry was standing there.

"Did you have these shipped in from somewhere?" she asked, knowing the answer before he spoke. Harry had sent for caviar and champagne, but his contribution to the ceremony was a massive bouquet of pink roses, already in full bloom. Amy knew their petals would become her marriage bed and, for all the time she'd spent exploding in Harry's arms, she was ready to give herself again.

"No," Harry answered, coming to her side and taking up one of the boughs with a frown. "I thought these were gone for the year."

Someday, Amy thought, she would tell him that white lilacs had been special to her and Tyler. Someday, she would say that Tyler had found a way to offer his blessing on their marriage, but now wasn't the time for explanations and Amy knew it.

She made a wreath of the lush lilacs for her hair, and when it came time for the ceremony, she drew a deep breath, said a prayer and went out to be married. Somehow, she would find a way to make Harry love her, truly love her, for real.

In the meantime, she would take whatever happiness she could find, wherever she found it.

The Ryans took Ashley and Oliver back to Seattle after the wedding, and Harry drove Amy to the jet. When the plane was high in the air, bound for some mysterious honeymoon destination, he left the pilot to handle the controls and joined Amy in the main cabin.

"You are beautiful, Mrs. Griffith," he said in a hoarse voice, taking off his suit jacket and draping it casually over the back of one of the seats. As he loosened his tie, he went on. "If you would be so good as to go into our bedroom and take off your clothes, please."

Amy could hear her own heartbeat, thundering as loudly as the jet's engines. "You're incredible," she said.

He smiled easily. "Thank you," he said, with a slight bow of his head.

Amy went to the master suite as she'd been bidden. The bed was mounded with pink rose petals, just as she'd expected, and there was a bottle of sparkling cider on the nightstand, cooling in a silver bucket.

"I thought champagne might be bad for the baby," Harry said from the doorway.

Amy was touched, but she wished she could matter to Harry as much as this child she was carrying. "Where are we going?"

Harry closed the door and kicked off his shoes. "I'm taking you to the morning star and back again," he said.

She couldn't believe it, not after the marathon they'd already put in. "I meant, for our honeymoon," she retorted dryly.

"Wait and see," he answered.

Soon rose petals were drifting down off the edges of the bed like pink rain, and Amy had made more than one trip to the morning star before the plane touched down.

She looked out and saw an isolated airstrip, a lot of desert and cactus and a proud hacienda of white stucco.

"Mexico?" she asked, kneeling on the bed and peering through the porthole.

"Yes," Harry answered, pulling her back down beside him.

Later, they went into the house, which was clean, well furnished and vacant. The pilot refueled the jet, went through a flight check and took off again.

"Is this your place?" Amy inquired, amazed. There was a pool out back, filled with inviting crystal-clear water, and the main bedroom had air-conditioning, a terrace and its own hot tub.

Harry smiled. "Belongs to a friend," he answered, setting their suitcases down at the foot of the massive bed. "Not a bad place to be a prisoner of love, is it?"

Amy blushed furiously at the reminder. "I gave in to your demands," she pointed out. "By all rights, I should no longer be classified as a captive."

"You may get a reprieve someday," Harry responded easily. "Time off for good behavior and all that. Louise is going to interview governesses for the kids so we can leave for the island soon."

Amy sat down on the bed. "You certainly are anxious to get back to Australia," she said, worried.

Harry stood near enough to touch the tip of her nose with an index finger. "Never fear, rose petal," he began. "I'm not planning to dump you and the nippers there and then go off and chase women. I want my baby to have the best possible start in life, and a calm, peaceful environment for its mother seems like a good beginning."

No protests came to mind. The kids, who would have been her best excuse for staying in Seattle, were eager to visit the island. Harry had promised them each a pony, and Tyler's folks were already making plans to visit.

The honeymoon lasted a week, though afterward those delicious days and nights ran together in Amy's mind, indiscernible from each other. She and Harry swam and made love, talked and made love, ate and made love, played tennis and made love.

Then they went back to Seattle, where Amy put her house on the market, said good-bye to her friends and family, packed summer things for herself and the children, put Rumpel into Mrs. Ingallstadt's loving care, and did her best to absorb the fact that her life had changed forever.

It wouldn't have been accurate to say she was unhappy—she was married to a man she loved desperately and was expecting his child—but there was an undercurrent of suspense. Harry was doing what he saw as his duty, and it didn't matter that he did such a damn good job at pretending to like it.

Amy's happiness was underlaid with a sense of urgency, of barely controlled anxiety.

The children thrived on the long, often-interrupted journey from Seattle to Australia. Both of them took their turns at the plane's controls, and when they stopped in Hawaii for a day, they explored their surroundings with energetic delight. The same thing happened in Fiji and Auckland, New Zealand and finally Sydney.

Once again, there was no problem with Customs. Ashley and Oliver were permitted into the country on the strength of Amy's passport and, she suspected, because Harry Griffith was their stepfather.

Returning to Harry's private isle, which Oliver promptly renamed Treasure Island, was like having the gates of Eden swing open again. It was a second chance.

The governess Louise had selected, a pretty brown-haired girl who had been doing graduate work at the University of Washington, was waiting when they arrived, as were Elsa and Shelt O'Donnell. Evidently, Amy thought testily, the nanny had taken a direct flight.

Although Amy's pregnancy was in its early stages, it had already begun to take its toll. She was exhausted from the trip to Australia, even though Harry had taken every opportunity to let her rest.

She hadn't been able to sleep on the plane, though she'd tried. Instead, she'd mindlessly read one book after another, and five seconds after she'd closed the last cover, she'd forgotten what the story was about. When she wasn't reading, she was in one of the swanky bathrooms, being violently sick.

Amy concluded that she just wasn't cut out to be a jet-setter.

When they finally reached their destination, she slept for two days straight, waking up only to eat and bathe and go to the bathroom, and although he was in bed beside her at regular intervals, Harry didn't once make love to her. She supposed the inevitable withdrawal had already begun, and for the first time in her life she was irrationally jealous of another woman.

Mary Anne, the governess, to be precise.

"You're just saying Louise hired her," Amy said pouting one night, when she and Harry were sitting on the terrace outside their room. The children were asleep and the sky was scattered with gaudy stars that were bigger and brighter than they had any business being. "You probably handpicked Mary Anne yourself, because of her great body."

Harry bent over her chair, gripping the arms, his nose less than an inch from Amy's. "You're very fortunate that you're pregnant, rose petal," he said. "If you weren't, I'd turn you over my knee, bare your backside and paddle you soundly for saying that."

Amy stuck out her lip. "You wouldn't dare. Modern American men don't do such things."

"Maybe they don't," Harry replied softly, "but I'm not an American and I'm not especially modern, either. It would behoove you to remember that."

A tear slipped down Amy's cheek. "She's so pretty."

With a warm chuckle, Harry gathered Amy up, sat down in the chair she'd occupied before, and cradled her on his lap. "If I didn't know better, Amy-girl," he said soothingly, holding her close, "I'd think Tyler did you wrong. What on earth gives you the idea that I'm constantly on the prowl for other women?"

"You wouldn't really spank a grown woman," Amy said, ignoring his question. But she laid her head against his shoulder, feeling fat and frumpy and very worried.

"Don't test the theory," Harry warned. "Australian men are still a generation or two behind the times, love. I would never get myself into a drunken rage and beat you or anything like that, but a few smart swats on the bottom never hurt."

"That depends on whose bottom it is," Amy reasoned. She had an unsettling feeling that Harry was totally serious.

Harry laughed and kissed her soundly on the forehead. "I will never, ever, be unfaithful," he promised in a sincere tone of voice a few moments later. "So stop worrying."

"What about when I'm fat and cranky and I'm retaining water?"

"You're cranky now, love, and no doubt you're retaining water, too." He opened her robe, baring one of her breasts to the attentions of an idle index finger. "And all I can think about is taking you to my bed and having you, thoroughly and well."

A delicious shudder ran through Amy, and when Harry bent to take her nipple between his lips and tease it mercilessly, she gasped.

Both her breasts were wet, their peaks hard and tingling, when Harry carried his bride inside and arranged her gently on his bed.

He laid aside her robe, like the wrapping on a gift, and never took his eyes from her as he stripped away his clothes.

He made her body tell all its secrets over the course of that magical night, and he had Amy so thoroughly and so well that, a couple of times, she thought she glimpsed the far side of forever.

Ten

The following week Harry left the island on business for the first time. Late that afternoon a tropical rainstorm blew in, hammering at the roof and tapping at the panes and making Ashley and Oliver rush, giggling with nervous excitement, from one window to another.

"Do you think it's a hurricane?" Amy asked Mary Anne, who was reading a book next to the fireplace. Amy had already come to terms with the fact that her children's teacher was a good person, not likely to engage in frolics with the master of the house, and the two women were becoming friends.

Mary Anne smiled. "Just a regular spring storm," she said.

It still seemed weird to Amy that mid-October could qualify as spring, but in Australia it did. "It doesn't appear to be bothering the kids."

Mary Anne closed her book, the pleasant expression lingering on her pretty face. "Kids are born adventurers," she agreed. "Is there anything I could get you, Mrs. Griffith? Some tea, maybe, or a glass of lemonade?"

Amy shook her head, feeling guilty for all the uncharitable thoughts she'd once harbored for this bright, intelligent young woman. "Thanks, no. I'm all right."

But she wasn't, and Mary Anne seemed to know that as well as Amy did. Amy was imagining Harry in cosmopolitan Sydney, dressed in one of his tuxedos, surrounded by sexy blondes, brunettes and redheads at some swanky party.

The next day, however, the storm blew out and Harry blew in. He brought fancy saddles for the kids, whose promised ponies had been waiting in the stable on their arrival, and for Amy there was a sketch pad and the biggest selection of colored chalk she'd ever seen.

She began to sketch the fabulous birds roosting in the trees just outside her walls. Startled at her own ability, Amy progressed to drawing images of Shelt and Elsa and Harry and the kids. When Ashley and Oliver were busy studying and Harry was either away or working, Amy's new interest in art positively consumed her.

Harry brought oil paints and canvases when he returned, and so many art books that Shelt had to make two trips to the landing strip to pick them all up.

In November, Amy and Harry went to Sydney on their own to take in a concert, have elegant dinners in gracious restaurants and do some preliminary shopping for the holidays. Amy visited her doctor, who pronounced her in good health, and she and Harry made love all of one afternoon and half the night.

When they returned to the island, Amy felt restored and renewed.

In early December they flew back to Sydney, this time taking Mary Anne and the kids with them. Although it was the height of summer, it was also Christmastime, and the clean, beautiful city was decorated for the holidays.

Harry and Amy took the kids and their governess to see *The Nutcracker* at one of the city's better theaters, then everyone shopped. Mary Anne sent presents to her family via airmail, and when they returned home, there were boxes galore awaiting them at the mainland post office.

They decorated a towering artificial tree, even though the sun was dazzlingly bright on the water. It seemed to Amy that there were presents hidden everywhere, and Ashley and Oliver were having the time of their lives.

Amy couldn't quite trust Harry's commitment—every time he left the island, she was on pins and needles until he returned. She had progressed by that point to making her own exquisite gift wrap, though, complete with hand-painted angels and other heralds of Christmas, and she did her level best to keep busy.

"Happy, love?" Harry asked, late Christmas Eve, when they'd filled the kids' stockings and played Santa.

Her emotions were complex and very confusing, and she supposed a lot of them could be ascribed to her pregnancy. For all of that, Amy was insecure as she had never been insecure before. Despite her art and her beautiful children and the much-wanted baby tucked away between her heart and her soul, Amy felt cut off from Harry. It seemed to her that the only time they were really close was when they were in the throes of lovemaking, unable to speak coherent words, flinging themselves at each other as if in battle.

Not being able to put her condition into words, Amy started to cry instead.

Harry put an arm around her and drew her close beside him in bed, one hand resting in a proprietary way on her rounded stomach. "There now, love," he said, his lips moving against her temple. "Your hormones are in a bit of a muddle, but it'll all come right in the end. You'll see."

Tell me you love me, Amy thought. "That's easy for you to say, Harry," she said aloud. "You're not pregnant."

"Darn good thing, too," he confirmed good-naturedly, "or we'd get nothing done for fending off photographers from all the tacky tabloids."

Amy laughed in spite of herself. "If I were you, I'd hate me," she said.

Harry rolled over to look deeply into her troubled eyes before he kissed her. "Hate you?" he countered hoarsely, after he'd left Amy dizzy from the intimacy of their contact. "Never."

Normally he would have made love to Amy then. Instead, he just cuddled her close, sighed contentedly and went to sleep.

The next day was a noisy riot of rumpled gift paper, food, presents and laughter.

On New Year's, Elsa and Mary Anne took the Christmas tree down and put it away, and Amy got out her oils and canvas and started to paint.

Harry took Amy to Sydney for another doctor's appointment at the end of the month and again in February.

The first week in March, just as winter was getting off to a fine Australian start, Amy went into labor.

This time she didn't go to the doctor, he came to her on board Harry's jet, bringing a nurse and an anesthesiologist with him.

Sara Tyler Griffith was born in her parents' bedroom, with a tropical storm threatening to make the seas run over onto the land. She was a lovely child, with the blue eyes all babies have, and a rich shock of dark, dark hair. Just as Ty had predicted.

Harry held his daughter, his beautiful eyes glistening with wondrous tears, while the doctor and nurse saw to Amy's care.

Amy looked at her husband and this innocent, trusting child, and couldn't help being happy, at least for the moment. She had practically everything she'd

ever wanted, and so what if there were slight imper-
fections in the fabric of her life? So what if Harry
didn't truly love her and she still wondered what he did
when he was away from home? Nobody had everything.

A day later, when her milk came in, Amy nursed
Sara, stroking her tiny, doll-like head, and told her,
"You'll be more your daddy's girl than mine, I think,
but I guess I can live with that." She smiled. "Just
between you and me, Sara Griffith, you'll be running
the family business someday. I have that on good au-
thority."

There was a timid knock at the door, and Ashley
and Oliver trailed in, drawn to their sister and at the
same time wondering how her presence would affect
their places in the scheme of things.

"I'm going to need lots and lots of help from the
two of you," Amy told her older children solemnly.
"Raising a baby is a very hard job, even if it is fun
most of the time, and I'm counting on you."

"What about Harry? Is he going to help?" Ashley
asked reasonably.

The words stung. Harry adored the baby, although
he seemed to hold just as high an affection for Ashley
and Oliver, but he'd already started drawing away
from Amy. He slept in one of the guest rooms, and
when he paid a visit, it was always to see his daughter,
not his wife. Soon he was traveling as much as ever,
and when Sara was two and a half months old, Amy's
unhappiness rose to tremendous proportions.

It was time, she decided when Harry called from Brisbane to say he'd be staying over a few days longer on business, for a confrontation.

Boldly Amy called the mainland and ordered a helicopter, since Harry had taken the jet. She kissed Ashley and Oliver goodbye and, carrying Sara while Shelt hauled the heavy diaper bag, she boarded the whirlybird and was soon on her way.

The pilot obligingly landed the copter on the roof of Harry's hotel, and not one but two bellhops were waiting to carry baggage.

"I'd like you to deliver our things to Room 373," Amy said to one of the young men, feeling more and more nervous as the elevator swept from the roof to the third floor. What was she doing?

If she caught Harry with another woman, she was going to be devastated. And if she didn't, he would be furious with her for not trusting him.

She bit her lower lip, holding Sara a little too tightly, when one of the bellhops knocked at the door of Harry's suite.

There was no answer, so the gentleman opened the door himself, using a special key, and escorted Amy inside.

Harry's clothes were hanging in the closet, but only Harry's clothes, and the dresser drawers contained his things alone. The scent of his cologne lingered in the air, but there was no tinge of perfume.

By that time Amy was beginning to feel really foolish. "I need to join one of those self-help groups for clingy women," she muttered to herself after the bellhops had taken their tips and left. She wanted to flee, to pretend she'd never done this stupid, suspicious, sneaky thing, but Sara was hungry and Amy herself was tired to the core of her spirit.

She lay down on the bed to nurse Sara, and she was lying there, half-asleep herself, when the door opened and Harry came in. Amy felt a pang when she saw the realization that she didn't trust him register in his wonderful indigo eyes.

"Well, Amy," he said, extending his arms from his sides in a gesture of furious resignation, "have you looked under the bed and checked the medicine cabinet for lipstick?"

Tears welled in her eyes. "I'm sorry," she said.

Harry bent to kiss his sleeping daughter's downy head, then took the infant and laid her gently in her portable crib. He had no kiss for Amy, however, only quiet, well-controlled outrage.

"What a pity you didn't come here because you wanted to be with me," he said bitterly. "Damn! I suppose you'll be hiring a private investigator next and having me followed!"

Amy sat up, trying to close her blouse, but Harry held her hands away, kneeling astraddle of her hips on the bed. He stared at her breasts for a long time, then, with a helpless groan, fell to her.

Because he hadn't touched her in so long, Amy was instantly on fire. And the anger pulsing in the room only made the interval more exciting.

Harry enjoyed one nipple, then the other, until he had Amy tossing helplessly on the bed. Then, with no more foreplay than that, he lifted Amy's cotton skirt and took her in one powerful stroke.

Amy gripped the underside of the headboard in both hands and held on, her back arched so high that only her head, shoulders, and heels were touching the bed. Her release began as Harry delved into her, and she went wild when he grasped her hips and bid her take him deeper and deeper.

Finally, with a burst of rasped swear words and an involuntary buckling of his body, Harry reached his climax.

Amy had been as thoroughly satisfied as he had, if not more so, and that was what made her next words so hard to say. "I'm leaving, Harry. I'm going back to the States."

Her husband was quiet for so long that Amy feared he hadn't heard her. On another level, she *hoped* he hadn't, so that she could back down, pretend she'd never voiced the decision.

Then, still inside her, he raised himself on his palms and glowered as he searched her eyes. *"What?"*

She tried to squirm out from under him, but he'd pinned her, and there was no going anywhere until he set her free.

"You were right before," she said with breathless misery. "We're not ready for marriage, either of us. You're angry and frustrated all the time, and I'm turning into a shrew. So I want to go home."

He searched her eyes with angry blue ones for a long, long moment. "You'll damn well leave Sara here if you do."

Amy shook her head. "I'll never walk away from my baby, Harry," she vowed.

Harry flung himself onto his back and glared up at the ceiling, his breathing ragged, his scowl black as clouds before a tropical storm. "Damn it all, woman, you would drive a saint to drink!"

"You're going to let us go?"

He turned to meet her eyes. "Not in a million years, love," he said, his voice totally void of all traces of affection, "but I will take you back to the lighthouse. Maybe a miracle will happen and you'll be the woman I married again."

His words hurt Amy almost as much as finding him in the middle of a romantic tryst would have. She turned onto her side and cried silently, her heart breaking as she listened to the roar of the shower, the familiar, once comforting sounds of a man dressing, the crisp closing of the door.

Sara, blissfully unaware that her parents were at war, slept undisturbed in her little bed.

Within the week, the family was back in the States and, a few days after their return, they were settled in the lighthouse. Ashley and Oliver were immediately enrolled in elementary school, and Mary Anne went back to her studies at the university. Harry spent all day, every day, in the city, throwing himself into his work, and sent a steady stream of aspiring housekeepers for Amy to interview.

She finally selected an English grandmother type, Mrs. Hobbs, because the woman reminded her of

Mrs. Ingallstadt. If nothing else, it was a relief not to have to review résumés and ask questions anymore.

"Main problem with you, mistress," Mrs. Hobbs announced one afternoon, when Amy was curled up in Harry's big leather chair, Sara nearly asleep at her breast, "is that you're tired. Begging your pardon, ma'am, but you've got dark circles under your eyes and every time I look at you, I want to cry because you seem so sad."

Amy gently lowered her daughter, put her bra in place and closed her blouse.

"I have everything," she confided forlornly. "It's shameful for me to feel so discontented."

"Maybe you should see your doctor," the gray-haired woman ventured kindly. "There are them as gets gloomy because there's chemicals off balance in their brain."

Smiling at the housekeeper's phrasing, Amy carried Sara to her crib and looked out the bedroom window at the choppy gray waters of Puget Sound. "I'm pretty sure my brain's all right," she said. *It's my heart that might not hold up.*

Mrs. Hobbs was puttering with the bedspread, even though it was mid-afternoon and the master suite was always the first room to be cleaned, after the kitchen. "Mr. Griffith be home tonight?" she asked casually.

Amy stiffened. How astute this Englishwoman was. She'd only been in the house a few days and already she knew there was trouble. "No," she said, hugging herself because she felt a chill. "Mr. Griffith won't be home. He has a late meeting tonight and conferences all day tomorrow."

The weekend ahead looked desolate from Amy's viewpoint: Ashley and Oliver would spend it with the Ryans on the mainland, and Harry, of course, would be working.

The housekeeper picked up the pink-and-gray plaid woolen afghan at the foot of the bed and refolded it, even though it had been perfectly arranged in the first place.

"Forgive me, ma'am," she said, lowering her eyes when Amy looked at her directly, "but it wouldn't hurt if you was to doll yourself up a little and spend some time in the city, with your husband."

Amy looked down at her baggy gray sweat suit, and a grin tugged at the corners of her mouth, even though she wanted very much to cry. "Are you insinuating that I'm not on the cutting edge of fashion, Mrs. Hobbs?"

The woman's already ruddy face was flushed with conviction. "Yes, ma'am."

The idea of going to Seattle, of perhaps finding some common ground with Harry, some way to reach him, was appealing. But Amy couldn't forget the last time she'd paid him an unscheduled visit, back in Brisbane. He'd been furious at her for mistrusting him.

"I have a small baby," Amy reminded Mrs. Hobbs and herself.

"She's big enough to be left for a day or so, ma'am. It's not like I haven't looked after a nipper or two in my time, you know. You'd just have to leave some milk."

Amy sighed. She could speak honestly to Mrs. Hobbs, and that was a great relief, because Amy had felt alone for a long time. "My husband wouldn't appreciate a visit from me," she admitted sadly, at the same time yearning to shop and see a play and eat in an elegant restaurant, all without having to nurse her baby or change a diaper. "He'd think I was checking up on him."

"That's easy to remedy," Mrs. Hobbs said briskly, fussing with the pillow shams. "You just play hard to get, Mrs. Griffith. You check into another hotel—not his—and then you call and leave a message, saying you're in town. After that, you go out and buy yourself some fine new clothes, and if it's a while before you return Mr. Griffith's messages when he calls, so much the better."

The plan appealed to Amy, whose unhappiness was rapidly escalating into sheer panic. Her marriage was turning out exactly as she had feared it would. If the relationship was to have any chance at all, she would have to stop mooning around and *do something*.

"You're right," she said excitedly. Then, impulsively, she gripped the housekeeper's sturdy shoulders and kissed her soundly on the cheek. "God bless you, Mrs. Hobbs, you're right!"

Amy packed hurriedly and made sure there was an ample supply of milk for Sara, who was already living mostly on baby food, anyway. When it was time for Ashley and Oliver to cross to West Seattle to meet their grandparents at the terminal, Amy kissed her infant daughter goodbye, rallied all her willpower, and got onto the ferry with them.

It wasn't easy; she and Sara had never been separated before, and the pull of maternal instinct was very strong indeed. In fact, a couple of times Amy thought she might not be able to keep herself from diving overboard and swimming back.

On the other hand, she wanted to reach out to Harry, to try to make things right between them again. She closed her eyes against a sudden swell of tears, remembering how he'd said he hoped a miracle would happen and she would turn back into the woman he'd married.

Am I so different? she wondered miserably, watching through blurred eyes as Oliver and Ashley ran happily up and down the deck on the other side of the window.

She looked down at herself.

Amy was only about five pounds heavier than she'd been before her pregnancy, but she *had* been neglecting her exercise program. She hadn't had a good haircut in weeks, and she often went for days without wearing makeup.

She felt a stirring of hope, because clothes and exercise and makeup and haircuts were all things within the realm of her control. Amy had read enough pop psychology to know she could change nothing about Harry, much less his feelings toward her, but she couldn't help hoping that he might be willing to meet her halfway.

After the boat docked and the Ryans had collected Ashley and Oliver, Amy drove downtown. Since Harry was staying in a suite at the Hilton, she took a room in the Towers at the Sheraton.

She called his office and left a message with the puzzled receptionist, who had offered to put her through to Harry immediately. "Just tell him I called," Amy said brightly, and then she hung up.

The phone was ringing fifteen minutes later when she was leaving the room, but Amy didn't stop to answer it. She knew Mrs. Hobbs wasn't calling about Sara because she'd just talked to the woman, and that left Harry.

Let him wonder, Amy thought, closing the door on the insistent jangling.

She walked to the nearby Westlake Center, an urban answer to the shopping mall, boasting several levels of good stores, and bought bath salts and special soaps and lotions at Crabtree & Evelyn. After that, Amy entered an upscale lingerie boutique called Victoria's Secret and purchased a sexy floral nightgown and some silky tap pants and camisoles.

Down the street from the mall, at Nordstrom, her favorite department store, Amy selected a black crepe sheath and a glittery jacket to match.

When Amy returned to her room to drop off her packages and hang up the dress and jacket, the message light on her phone was blinking. She dialed the registration desk and was told that Mr. Griffith had called twice, once from his office, once from his hotel. He'd left both numbers, as if Amy wouldn't know them.

"Thank you," Amy said with a smile. Then she took the elevator down to the lobby, had her hair cut and styled in the swanky hotel salon and charged the whole obscene price to Harry's American Express card.

On her return, Amy found two message envelopes just inside the door. Both were from Harry.

Feeling better all the time, and blessing Mrs. Hobbs for a genius, Amy yawned, set the messages aside and rustled through the Crabtree & Evelyn bag for her soap and bath salts. She indulged in a long, luxurious soak in the tub, ignoring the telephone when it rang. She and Mrs. Hobbs had worked out a system earlier; if the housekeeper needed to reach Amy for any reason, she would ring twice, hang up and ring twice again.

Amy must have fallen asleep for a little while, because the bathwater got cold. She was just reaching out to turn the spigot marked Hot when she heard the outer door open.

"Thanks, mate," she heard Harry say.

"Thank *you,* sir," a bellhop replied, obviously receiving a big tip for letting Harry into the room. Amy wondered if it was the cute one who looked a little like Bruce Willis.

"I think I'll complain to the management," Harry announced, stepping into the bathroom just as Amy was rising, towel wrapped, from the tub. "I could have been anybody, but all I had to do was tell them I was your husband.''

Amy smiled, though she felt almost as nervous as she had the first time she'd met Harry Griffith. "I told the concierge to keep an eye out for you," she admitted. Then she made a shooing gesture with one hand. "Get out of here, please. I want to dress."

"It's not like I've never seen you naked," Harry reasoned, frowning. He was leaning back against the sink counter, his arms folded, his dark brows drawn together. "What are you trying to do, Amy?"

She put a hand to his arm and eased him through the doorway. "I'm planning to have a luxurious dinner and see a play. Tomorrow I plan to shop."

Amy closed the door and locked it.

"You're doing all this alone?" Harry called from beyond the barrier.

"Yes," Amy answered, smiling at her reflection in the mirror. She liked her sleek new haircut; it made her look both sexy and mischievous. She waited a few beats before adding, "Unless, of course, you'd like to accompany me. I wouldn't want you to think I was crowding you, or checking up on you, or anything like that."

"Amy, this is silly. Open the door!"

Amy reached for a makeup sponge and a new bottle of foundation and leaned toward the mirror. "I'm busy," she chimed. "Maybe you could come back later."

"Damn it, I'll break this thing down if you don't let me in."

"You wouldn't do that," Amy reasoned, blending her foundation skillfully with the sponge. "Trashing a hotel room would definitely be unHarrylike. Besides, the management would be furious."

She heard him sag against the door, probably in exasperation, and her heart took wings. Maybe he didn't love her in the classical sense, maybe his attachment to her was largely sexual, but there was no denying that Harry cared.

When she turned the knob, he practically fell into the bathroom. Staring at her in angry bewilderment, he said, "I don't like being kept from my own wife."

"Tough," Amy replied, bending close to the mirror to begin applying her eye shadow. "I'm through walking on eggshells, Harry. I'm going to live my life, with or without your approval."

He filled the doorway, glowering, a human storm cloud. "What about Sara? Where does she fit into your plans, Mrs. Griffith? And where is she, by the way?"

"Sara is with Mrs. Hobbs. She's going to be one of those modern babies who goes everywhere with her mommy. I'll buy a carrier of some sort."

"Right. And when she gets hungry, you can just whip out a breast in the middle of a board meeting!" Obviously Harry was losing his perspective as well as his temper. He shoved a hand through his hair, making it unperfect. "Damn it, Amy, you can forget the whole crazy idea! You're not dragging my daughter through the corporate world like a rag doll!"

Amy finished shadowing her right eye and started on her left. "Actually I was thinking in terms of attending art school. I've got real talent, you know, and in this day and age, a woman needs to know how to support herself."

Harry, the cool, the calm, the collected man of the nineties, looked as if he were going to pop an artery. His voice, when he spoke, was low and lethal. "Even if you didn't have me to look after you, Amy, you would never need a job. Between what Tyler left you and the proceeds from selling the house—"

"There are other reasons to work besides money," Amy said, reaching for a green kohl pencil and starting to line her eyes. "Like knowing you mean something, knowing you're strong and you're interesting and you're worth something all on your own. The subject isn't open to debate, Harry—I'm going to art school, whether you like it or not."

Out of the corner of her eye, Amy could see that her husband's jaw was clamped down tight, as though he'd just bitten through a piece of steel. "Fine," he said. And when the door of the hotel room slammed, Amy wondered if her wonderful plan had backfired.

Eleven

Harry paused in the doorway of his office, his hand still on the light switch, thinking he'd finally lost his mind, once and for all.

He blinked, looked again and, sure as hell, Tyler was there, sitting in Harry's leather chair, feet propped on the tidy surface of his antique desk.

"You're really seeing me," his friend assured him with a sigh. Ty's hands were cupped at the back of his head, and he looked pretty relaxed for someone who'd been dead in the neighborhood of three years.

Harry rubbed his eyes with one hand. It was the problems with Amy that had pushed him over the brink, he was certain of that. "This is ridiculous," he said.

Tyler sighed again and hoisted his feet down from Harry's desk. He was wearing clothes Harry vaguely remembered: jeans and a University of Washington sweatshirt. "Look, old buddy, I don't have all night here, so listen up. I had to get special permission from the head office to make this appearance, and this is positively the last time they'll let me come back. You're blowing it, man."

Harry went to his private bar and poured himself a brandy. A good, stiff drink might jump-start his brain circuits and blast him back to reality.

When he turned around, however, Tyler was as substantially *there* as ever. He was leaning against the edge of the desk now, his arms folded, his eyes full of pitying fury.

"Do you realize what you have?" the apparition demanded. "Amy is wonderful and sweet and bright, and damn it, she loves you! There must be a million guys out there—" Tyler gestured toward the bank of windows behind the desk "—just wishing to God they could meet somebody like her! She adores you, you lucky bastard!"

Harry shoved one hand through his hair, thinking what a remarkable mechanism the human mind is. He would have sworn his dead friend was really standing there, every bit as real as Amy or the janitor downstairs dust mopping the lobby, or the doorman out on the street.

"Wrong," he said forcefully. "Amy's planning to leave me and become some kind of barefoot Bohemian, painting pictures and carrying my daughter around on her back like a papoose.''

Tyler laughed, and the effect was remarkably authentic. It gave Harry a pang, remembering the old days, when he and Ty had thought the whole world was funny. ''Oh, the art school thing,'' Tyler said. ''As you Aussies say, 'No worries, mate.' ''

The game was becoming alarmingly easy to play, and Harry put his brandy aside, unfinished. ''You mean, she's going to change her mind about art school?''

''Hell, no,'' Tyler answered with a cocky grin. ''You really started something when you gave her those art supplies—even Amy didn't know she had a talent for painting. In three years she'll be having her own shows in some of the best galleries in the country.''

Harry sagged into a chair. Damn, but this was elaborate. He hadn't known he was harboring so many possibilities in his subconscious mind. ''And that's supposed to keep me from worrying?'' he muttered. He'd already had a sample of the new Amy, the woman who was bent on living her life to the fullest, with or without him, and he wasn't sure he liked her. One thing he had to admit, though, she was exciting.

''Relax,'' Tyler said. He crossed the room to touch one of the crystal liquor decanters on Harry's bar. Harry figured a genie would probably come out of the thing, thus laying to rest all doubt that Harry had lost his sanity. ''Amy's becoming the person she's supposed to be, and you'll be a world-class fool if you try to stand in her way.''

"How," Harry began raggedly, closing his eyes, "am I supposed to live without her? Tell me that."

"You won't have to live without Amy if you'll just quit trying to drive her away," Tyler replied without missing a beat.

Harry's eyes flew open. "I haven't been trying to drive her away!" he hollered.

Tyler grinned indulgently. "Sure you have, Harry. You're afraid to let go of your emotions and really care about Amy and the kids because of what happened before, in your first marriage."

A sense of bleakness swept over Harry, practically crushing him. He'd had such high hopes back then, for himself and Madeline and little Eireen, before he'd learned just how cruelly unpredictable life can be.

"I see you're not trying to deny that," Tyler observed, pacing back and forth a few feet in front of Harry, his hands clasped behind his back. Except for the clothes, this was probably the way his friend had looked in the courtroom, authoritative and confident.

But not dead, of course.

"You're not here."

"Amy kept saying that, too. Did you like the white lilacs I sent for the wedding?"

Harry's mouth dropped open, but he didn't speak because he couldn't.

"Look," Tyler said, beginning to summarize, "I don't really give a damn whether you believe I'm here or not, because what you think about me doesn't matter. But you and Amy have to make it work— there's a lot riding on it.''

For the first time since his friend's death, Harry thought he might actually break down and weep. He loved Amy, thoroughly, totally, as he'd never loved another human being, but Tyler had been right earlier. He was terrified of letting his guard down completely where Amy was concerned, because losing her would kill him.

"You'll find her in front of the Fifth Avenue Theater," Tyler said. He was standing at the windows now, looking through the shutter slats at the city lights. "She's carrying an extra ticket in her purse and hoping against hope that you'll have the good sense to show up. Don't drop the ball, Harry. Don't lose her.''

"Next," Harry sighed, "you're going to offer to show me how the world would be if I'd never been born, right?''

Tyler chuckled. "Sorry, that's a Christmas bit. Good-bye, Harry, and good luck.''

Before Harry's very eyes, Tyler vanished. He was there, then he wasn't. It was weird.

Harry got his coat and wandered out of the office, through the swanky reception area and over to the elevators. He rubbed his chin as he waited, then looked at his watch.

It was seven-ten, and curtain time at the theater was usually eight o'clock. His hotel was connected with the theater by a walkway—

She *had* said she was going to the theater.

That was how he knew, Harry was sure of it. He'd only imagined Tyler because he was so stressed out, so lonesome for his wife. It was a spiritual longing, as well as a physical one, intense enough to explain his hallucinations.

He went back to the Hilton, glanced at the telephone—the message light wasn't blinking—and then took a hot shower. He shaved and put on fresh clothes, and when he passed through the underground shopping center and climbed the stairs to the Fifth Avenue Theater, Amy was standing there on the sidewalk.

She was so beautiful, in her clingy black dress, sexy jacket and high heels, that Harry was momentarily immobilized by the sight of her. He just stood gaping at her, his hand gripping the stair railing.

Amy must have felt his gaze, because she turned and smiled, and Harry tightened his grasp on the railing, as much off balance as if he'd been punched in the stomach.

"Hello, Harry," she said gently.

"You really mean it, about this art school thing?"

Worry flickered in her hopeful eyes. "I really mean it," she confirmed softly.

He finally broke his inertia and joined her in the line of theatergoers waiting to be admitted.

"You look fantastic," he said, not quite meeting her eyes.

He could feel her smile, warm as sunlight. "Thanks, Harry. You look pretty good yourself."

He turned, unable to resist the pull anymore, and went tumbling, head over heels into her eyes.

She linked her arm with his. "I love you, Harry," she said.

Harry felt something steely and cold melt within him. "And I love you," he whispered raggedly.

They went into the theater with the crowd, and sat there in their seats, holding hands. Harry was never able to remember, without a reminder from Amy, what play they saw that night, because his mind was everywhere but on the stage.

After the final curtain, they had a late dinner at an expensive, low-key restaurant.

Harry felt as nervous as a kid on his first date.

He wondered what she would say if he told her she wasn't the only one who'd ever had a delusion, that he'd seen Tyler, too.

"I think I'm going round the bend," he finally confessed, because he wanted to be honest with Amy. Completely honest.

She arched one delicate brow and took a sip of her wine. "Oh? Why is that?"

"Because when I went back to the office after our conversation in your room, fully intending to lick my wounds and whimper a little, Tyler was there."

Amy set the wineglass down, very slowly. Her cheeks were pale, and although her throat worked visibly, no sound passed her lips.

"Not that I believe I saw a ghost or anything like that," Harry was quick to clarify.

Amy reached for her wineglass again, her hand shaking as she extended it. She closed her eyes and took three or four gulps before looking at Harry squarely again and agreeing, "Of course not."

Harry sighed. "The human mind is a fascinating thing," he ruminated, hedging.

"What did Tyler want?" Amy asked in a small voice.

"He delivered a lecture, essentially," Harry said, frowning, "and I must confess that he was pretty much on target. Obviously my subconscious mind had worked the whole thing out beforehand."

"Obviously," Amy said in a whisper. Her beautiful eyes were very wide, and Harry could see the pulse at the base of her throat.

It made him want to kiss her there, as well as a few other places.

"I've been a fool, Amy," he went on, after clearing his throat and shifting uncomfortably in his chair. "I thought I could keep myself from loving you, and thereby keep my heart from being broken to bits, but it didn't work. Practically every stroke of good fortune in my life can be traced back to you—not only did you give me yourself, but Ashley and Oliver and Sara, too. God in heaven, Amy, I love you more than I ever believed could be possible, and it hurts—and I'm scared."

Tears brimmed in her eyes, and she reached across the table to grip Harry's hand. "Me, too. Everything just sort of fell into place with Tyler—we met, we got married, we had kids. I was happy, and I think he was, as well. Then I met you and suddenly everything was complicated."

Harry lifted her hand to his lips and kissed the knuckles lightly. A bittersweet sense of homecoming filled him. It was not like returning after an hour's absence, or even a week's. No, it was as though an eternity had passed, during which he'd been deprived of this woman he needed more than air, more than light, more than water.

"Give me a second chance," he said. "I'm a chauvinist, but I can reform."

Amy laughed softly. "Don't reform too much. There are things I like about the caveman approach."

Harry raised his eyebrows. "Such as?"

"Such as being your love prisoner," Amy said, leaning closer and uttering the words in a breathless tone that made Harry's loins pulse and his heart start to hammer.

"Is it warm in here?" he inquired, tugging at his collar.

Amy's smile was slow and hot and saucy. He felt her toe make a slow foray up his pant leg. "Steaming," she answered.

Harry practically tore his wallet from his inside pocket, fished out a credit card, and threw it at the first waiter to pass by. They were out of the hotel and onto the bustling night streets within minutes.

"My place or yours?" Amy teased.

"Which is closer?"

"Mine."

"Yours it is."

They entered Amy's room a few minutes later, and she snatched up a shopping bag and immediately disappeared into the bathroom again.

Harry paced, listening as the water ran and the toilet flushed and various things clinked and rattled. Finally he paused outside the door. "Amy?"

"Be patient, Harry."

He tried, he honestly tried. He went to the telephone and ordered champagne, then called the hotel florist for a dozen of whatever flower they happened to have on hand.

Both the carnations and the champagne arrived before Amy came out of the bathroom, but the wait was worth it. She was wearing a gossamer floral nightgown, of the very thinnest silk, and it clung to her womanly curves in a way that made Harry's heart surge into his throat.

"My God," he rasped.

Amy walked past him, her hips swaying, her soft skin exuding the scent of lavender. The bellhop had opened the champagne before leaving the room, and Amy poured a glass for herself and one for Harry.

"Let's offer a toast," she said, holding out his glass.

He accepted it with a slightly unsteady hand.

"To us," she said. "To you and me and Ashley and Oliver and little Sara—and whoever else might happen to come along in the next couple of years."

Harry swallowed. "You mean, you're willing to have another child? But you've been so tired, and there's art school—"

"Other women have done it. I'll manage, Harry, with a lot of help from you and Mrs. Hobbs."

Now it was Harry who had tears in his eyes. He set his champagne aside and laid his hands on Amy's waist, pulling her close to him. "God, Amy, how I love you," he breathed.

She put down her glass, slid her arms around his neck, and drove him crazy by wriggling against him.

"Prove it," she said.

"Oh, I will," he answered.

Harry was as good as his word. He buried his fingers in Amy's hair and gently but firmly pulled her head back for his kiss. When his mouth crushed hers and his tongue gained immediate entry, Amy nearly fainted. It had been so long.

She peeled off Harry's jacket while their tongues battled, then wrenched at his tie and ripped open his shirt, sending little buttons flying in every direction.

Amy didn't care about shirt buttons. She pushed the fabric savagely aside, sought a masculine nipple with her tongue and nibbled until Harry was moaning under his breath.

"This time," she said, "you're *my* prisoner. You have to do everything I tell you, and give me everything I want."

Harry moaned as she unfastened his belt buckle. "Amy—"

"I want to hear you crying out, for once," Amy said, kissing her way down his belly, baring his navel. "I want to hear you beg, the way I always do."

"Ooooh," he rasped, as she knelt and pushed down his slacks, her hands moving strong and light on his buttocks, molding and shaping him, pushing him into the pleasure she so willingly offered.

Amy enjoyed her husband, and the beautiful, angry, hungry sounds he was making, and she was greedy about it. His firm flanks began to flex under her palms and, with a gasp, he leaned forward to brace himself against the dresser.

Amy granted him no quarter.

"Amy..." he pleaded, a man in delirium. "Oh, God, Amy, I'm going to—"

She stopped, just long enough to finish the sentence for him, and then she was insatiable again.

Harry stiffened, with a low, primitive cry, and she made him experience every nuance, every degree of sensation, every shade of ecstasy. When she finally released him, it was clear that he could barely stand.

Their clothes were mysteriously gone. Amy didn't remember shedding her own garments or stripping away Harry's, but when they fell onto the big bed in the center of the room, they were both naked.

"I'll have to have vengeance for that," Harry said, after a long time, rolling onto his side to begin kissing Amy's stomach.

"For what?" Amy teased, but a little gasp of anticipation betrayed her as Harry's mouth drew dangerously near the center of her femininity.

"For turning me inside out," Harry answered in a rumbling voice, burrowing through the moist delta that protected Amy's womanhood to take her boldly into his mouth.

She cried out, but it was only the beginning. Harry teased her unmercifully, for what seemed like hours.

Amy was wild, untamed, primitive in her responses. She cried, she pleaded, she moaned and groaned and cursed, and finally, in a long, shattering spasm, she lost all control.

Although he had what he wanted, Harry was not a benevolent captor.

He folded her close, and held her, and stroked her, until she was ready again. When he entered her, it was a sudden, fierce invasion, and her eyes rolled back in her head.

"Look at me, Amy," he ordered.

She opened her eyes and stared up at her husband dreamily.

"I want to see you responding to me," Harry said. "I want to see you belonging to me . . ."

Amy dug her heels into the bed and rose and fell under Harry with graceful desperation. She needed him, wanted him, so much, that giving herself was heaven. "Put a baby inside me, Harry," she choked out. "Please—give me your baby."

At her words, he seemed to lose control. He groaned and threw his head back, as fierce as a stallion having his mare. "I love you, Amy," he struggled to say.

She ran her hands up and down the straining muscles of his back, soothing, tormenting, urging him on. "I love you," she answered breathlessly, meeting him thrust for thrust, heartbeat for heartbeat, dream for dream.

Finally, in one blinding, spectacular collision, the joyous miracle happened and their two souls mated, just as their bodies did.

Later, much later, Amy lay with her head on Harry's shoulder, exhausted, nibbling at his heated skin.

"We never made love in the tree house again," she said, as he entwined one finger in a lock of her hair.

Harry drew in a deep breath, let it out slowly. "If ever I've heard a good reason for going back to Australia, that's it. We'll leave as soon as Oliver and Ashley are out of school."

Amy smiled in the cozy darkness and kissed Harry's shoulder. "And come back before classes start at my art school," she negotiated.

"Deal," he said, after a lengthy and very philosophical sigh.

Down on the sidewalk, beside the hotel, stood Tyler, unseen by the city dwellers hurrying past him, looking up at one certain window. He was about to return to a place where there was no darkness and no pain, but during those few precious moments, he was a living, breathing man again.

He could hear the noise of passing cars, a plane overhead, people chattering as they rushed along. He felt the solid cement of the sidewalk beneath his feet and smelled the peculiar mix of salt water, pine and exhaust fumes that was Seattle. He also felt no small measure of satisfaction because he knew Harry and Amy had a long, rich life ahead of them.

Tyler had accomplished his mission. Amy and Harry would live and love, laugh and cry. They would decorate Christmas trees together and balance checkbooks and shop for studded snow tires. They would fight sometimes, but they would have a glorious time making up.

It was all written in the book.

Tyler sighed and lifted one hand in farewell. "Good-bye," he whispered. And then he walked away, into the waiting light.

One year later...

The tree house was just as Amy remembered it, dusty and primitive and wonderful. Harry gave her a mischievous pinch on the bottom as she climbed the last rung and scrambled inside.

It had taken them a little longer than they'd expected to reach this very special, very private place—Amy had completed her classes at the art school, and she worked on her painting for several hours every day.

Sitting there, with her blue-jeaned legs drawn up, she made a mental note to draw a sketch of the tree house. She would frame the picture, and when she and Harry and the kids were far away in the States, she could look at the drawing and remember.

"I think you're crazy, wanting to spend the night here," Harry remarked, dusting off his corduroy pants. "If the mosquitoes don't eat us alive, the rain will come through and give us our deaths."

Amy laughed. "Me, Jane," she said. "You, Tarzan. And don't you forget it, buster!"

Harry opened the canvas bag he'd brought along, taking out food, a blanket and a small sterno-powered stove. "Alas," he said, "all we need now is a monkey."

Amy's smile was broad; she could feel it stretching her face. She waited for Harry to look up and see her kneeling there, beaming, and laid her hands to her flat stomach. "We already have three monkeys," she answered. "I guess one more won't hurt."

Harry's befuddled expression made her shriek with laughter, scaring all the beautiful birds from their roosts in the tree.

When the beating of wings finally died down, he said, "You mean, you're—?"

"Again." Amy nodded. "I think it's a boy this time."

Harry swallowed visibly, scrambled over to her and covered both her hands with one of his own, as though by doing that he could somehow make contact with this new child. His indigo eyes glistened with tears of wonder.

Amy rose up on her haunches to kiss Harry's eyelids, first one and then the other. She tasted his tears.

"Do you know how much I love you, Harry Griffith?" she asked, one hand on either side of his handsome face.

His voice was gruff. "How much?" he asked.

Her answer was a kiss, deep and fiery. "That much," she said, when it was over.

Harry broke away to spread the blanket on the floor of the tree house. His motions were graceful and quick, and when he reached for Amy, she came to him willingly, with laughter and love and the purest joy.

He kissed her, subjecting her to a tender invasion of his tongue, and then laid her on the blanket and began removing her clothes with deft, methodical hands.

"I can't wait, Amy," he said, tossing her jeans aside and bending her knees and pushing her legs wide of each other. "I've got to be inside you, part of you, now."

She opened his jeans, pushed them down, along with his briefs. "Come in, Mr. Griffith," she whispered.

In the depths of the night, the rain came.

Harry lay awake on the floor of the tree house, listening, holding a sleeping Amy close by his side. He supposed he should wake her and insist that they go back to the shelter and safety of their house on the other island, but he didn't have the heart to awaken his wife. She was tired and she'd given him everything and she looked like an angel, lying there.

Idly, he caressed her. Soon, her beautiful body would ripen, her breasts would grow heavy with milk to nourish his child. He smiled, even though his vision was suspiciously blurred. He wondered if Amy would be as crabby this time around as she'd been while she was carrying Sara.

He decided he didn't care.

She moved against him, inadvertently setting him on fire again. Some men were put off by pregnancy, he knew, but knowing Amy was going to bear a child—his child—made him yearn for her in a way that went beyond the physical into a realm he didn't begin to understand.

"Harry?"

He kissed her temple. "Shhh, it's all right. Sleep."

She played with his nipples and the hair on his stomach. "Harry?" Her tone was serious.

"Mmm?"

"Are you happy about the new baby? Really happy?"

"Ecstatic," he answered.

"Oliver says if he doesn't get a brother pretty soon, he's joining the Foreign 'Region.' "

Harry laughed. Oliver was a miniature version of Ty, and Harry loved the boy as much as if he'd been his own, by blood. "Promises, promises," he said.

"You've been so good to them, Harry—Ashley and Oliver, I mean. Anyone would think they were as much yours as Sara is."

"They *are* as much mine. In a funny sort of way, I think Tyler gave them to me. He knew I could be trusted to love his children as deeply as he did."

She sniffled against his shoulder. "I really saw him," Amy said half to herself after a long moment had passed.

"So did I," admitted Harry, who had long since come to terms with the fact that Tyler had really been in his office that night, when Harry's and Amy's marriage had been in crisis.

"Do you think Ty's happy, wherever he is?"

Harry thought the question through, even though he'd done as much many, many times before.

"Yes, rose petal," he said sincerely. "He's happy."

Amy raised her head far enough to plant a row of tantalizing kisses along Harry's jawline. "I think I just felt a raindrop land on my backside," she said.

Harry chuckled and gave said backside an affectionate squeeze. "I love a sophisticated woman," he replied.

Amy nudged him with one elbow, pretending to be angry. "Oh, yeah?" she joked. "What's her name?"

*   *   *   *   *

NEW YORK BLOCKBUSTER SWEEPSTAKES
OFFICIAL RULES—NO PURCHASE NECESSARY

To enter, complete an Official Entry Form or 3" x 5" card by hand printing the words "New York Blockbuster Sweepstakes" and your name and address thereon and mailing it in the U.S. to: New York Blockbuster Sweepstakes, P.O. Box 9076, Buffalo, NY 14269-9076, or in Canada to: New York Blockbuster Sweepstakes, P.O. Box 637, Fort Erie, Ontario L2A 5X3. Limit: One entry per outer mailing envelope. Entries must be received no later than 1/31/97. No liability is assumed for lost, late, damaged, nondelivered or misdirected mail. Entries are void if they are in whole or in part illegible, incomplete or damaged.

One winner will be selected in a random drawing to be conducted no later than 2/28/97 from among all eligible entries received. Prize consists of a 3 day/2 night weekend for two (Friday-Sunday) including round-trip air transportation from commercial airport nearest winner's home, two nights hotel accommodations (one room double occupancy), at the New York Marriott Marquis Hotel, and a pair of theater tickets to a major Broadway show (approx. prize value: $2,400 U.S.). Travelers must provide their own transportation to and from the commercial airport nearest winner's home; are responsible for taxes, tips and incidentals; must execute and return a Release of Liability prior to travel; and must depart and return prior to 12/31/97.

Sweepstakes offer is open only to residents of the U.S. (except Puerto Rico) and Canada who are 18 years of age or older, except employees and immediate family members of Harlequin Enterprises, Limited, their affiliates, subsidiaries, and all agencies, entities and persons connected with the use, marketing or conduct of this sweepstakes. All federal, state, provincial, municipal and local laws apply. Offer void wherever prohibited by law. Taxes and/or duties are the sole responsibility of the winner. Any litigation within the province of Quebec respecting the conduct and awarding of prize may be submitted to the Régie des alcools des courses et des jeux. Prize is guaranteed to be awarded; winner will be notified by mail. No substitution for prize is permitted. Odds of winning are dependent on the number of eligible entries received. Potential winner must sign and return an Affidavit of Eligibility within 30 days of notification. In the event of non-compliance within this time period, prize may be awarded to an alternate winner. If prize or prize notification is returned as undelivered, prize may be awarded to an alternate winner. By acceptance of his/her prize, winner consents to use of his/her name, photograph or likeness for the purpose of advertising, trade and promotion on behalf of Harlequin Enterprises, Limited, without further compensation unless prohibited by law. In order to win a prize, a resident of Canada will be required to correctly answer a time-limited arithmetical skill-testing question by mail.

For the name of the winner (available after 3/31/97), send a separate stamped, self-addressed envelope to: New York Blockbuster Sweepstakes 4815 Winner, P.O. Box 4200, Blair, NE 68009-4200 U.S.A.

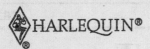 

NYTrule-R

Win an exciting weekend for two in New York City at the

NEW YORK

MARQUIS

including return airfare and tickets
to a Broadway Show!

You and a guest could be on your way to the
Big Apple, courtesy Harlequin Enterprises
and the New York Marriott Marquis! See
Official Sweepstakes Rules for more details.

NEW YORK BLOCKBUSTER SWEEPSTAKES
OFFICIAL ENTRY FORM

To enter, complete an Official Entry Form or a 3" x 5" card by hand printing "New York
Blockbuster Sweepstakes," your name and address, and mail to: **in the U.S.:** New York
Blockbuster Sweepstakes, P.O. Box 9076, Buffalo, NY 14269-9076, or **in Canada:**
New York Blockbuster Sweepstakes, P.O. Box 637, Fort Erie, Ontario, L2A 5X3. Limit one entry
per outer mailing envelope. Entries must be received no later than 1/31/97. No liability is
assumed for lost, late, damaged, nondelivered or misdirected mail.

NEW YORK BLOCKBUSTER SWEEPSTAKES
OFFICIAL ENTRY FORM

Name: _____

Address: _____

City: _____

State/Province: _____

Zip/Postal Code: _____

KNL

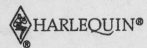

NYTentry

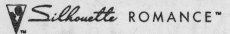

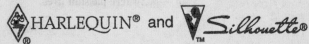

Add a double dash of romance to your
festivities this holiday season
with two great stories in

Christmas Celebration

Featuring full-length stories by bestselling authors

Kasey Michaels
Anne McAllister

These heartwarming stories of love triumphing
against the odds are sure to add some extra
Christmas cheer to your holiday season. And this
distinctive collection features **two full-length novels,**
making it the perfect gift at great value—for
yourself or a friend!

Available this December at your favorite retail outlet.

Silhouette®

...where passion lives.

XMASCEL